OFF LIMITS

CORRUPT COWBOYS

BOOK ONE

EMMA CREED

Off Limits
Copyright 2023 by Emma Creed
All Rights Reserved
First Edition

No part of this book may be reproduced or transmitted in any form or by any means, electronic or mechanical, including photocopying, recording, or by any information storage and retrieval system without written permission of the author, except for the use of brief quotations in a book review.

This is a work of fiction. Names, characters, businesses, places, events and incidents are either the product of the author's imagination or used in a fictitious manner. Any resemblance to actual persons, living or dead, actual events, or locales is entirely coincidental. The use of any real company and/or product names is for literary effect only. All other trademarks and copyrights are the property of their respective owners.

Cover design by: Rebel Ink Co
Interior design by: Rebel Ink Co
Editing by: Yvette Mitchell
Proofreading By: Andrea Stafford

AUTHOR NOTE

Off Limits and all books in the Corrupt Cowboys series are a work of fiction and contain adult content. Due to the nature of the series you should expect to come across various subject matter that some readers may find disturbing, and it is intended for readers 18+

Please contact the author if you have any questions.

OFF LIMITS
CORRUPT COWBOYS BOOK ONE

CHAPTER 1

GARRETT

"Tell him he's crazy," I look at my brother and wait for him to have my back on this.

"I'm with Garrett on this one, Pops." Cole gives his answer, and our father shakes his head in disappointment.

"Half the herd have been taken, and we know exactly who's behind it. If you go the official route and put in a complaint, I guarantee those cattle will be over the border by tomorrow. Give me five men from the bunkhouse, and I'll have 'em back by tonight."

"There's no way you're getting that livestock back without a fight." Pops creases his brow, the way he always does when he's thinking something over.

"Oh, I fully intend on it. You think I'm just going to get our livestock back? I'm gonna teach those rustlers a lesson."

"And how do you suppose you'll find them?" Our old man sits back in his leather chair and folds his arms. He thinks he's got me beat, but he's wrong.

"I've heard Trevor Henson takes his cut from the rustlers. He's what they call a fixer, and I *do* know where to find *him*. I got Finn and Tate on standby, waiting to ride into town to pick him up."

"Pick him up?" Pops' eyebrows raise sarcastically.

"Yeah, they'll take him out to the line camp so I can talk with him."

"What kinda talk are you thinking of havin'?" Pops may disapprove of it, but he's fully aware of the kinda shit that goes down at the line camp.

"Well, that'll all depend on Trevor, and how willing he is to share his information." I shrug.

"Call off the boys. I'll contact the commissioner and have him send an agent to speak to Trevor." Pops' order makes me even more savage. It's exactly why our family is failing. The old man needs to stop being so stubborn and find the sense in what I'm saying. But instead, he rolls his eyes and lights himself a cigar, acting like us losing fifty grand worth of cattle ain't an issue. How the fuck am I supposed to drag us out the hole he's put us in when this is his attitude? With Pops everything is financial. He measures a man's power by his bank balance.

This family used to run Fork River. Thirty years ago, no-one would have *dared* steal our livestock because we were feared.

And that's how I measure a man's power.

By those who fear him.

"Pops, I get your morals, and I know you like to stay above the law, but times are changing, and we can't get left behind. No one plays by the rules anymore, and if we don't react to this, it's gonna be us that gets hit every single time." I tap my finger on his desk to emphasize each of my words.

Cole remains leant against the wall, waiting on Pops' reaction. He's never scared to get his hands dirty, same as our other brother Wade. Sometimes I have to wonder how we ended up the way we are, when we got a man like Bill Carson for a father.

"Let me take care of this." I take a calming breath and try one last attempt to get him seeing sense. I'm not afraid to throw it all at the wall. This ranch has been part of our family for over 100 years. These valleys and trees ain't known nothing other than Carsons, and as long as I'm breathing, that's how it will stay.

"And, supposing there ain't five men in the bunkhouse prepared to risk their lives for half a herd?" He tries to be smart and fails. Mitch, who runs the bunkhouse, is on my level, and ever since my old man put me in charge of the hiring and firing, I can guarantee I got five men willing and waiting.

"Trust me. This will be Saturday night entertainment for those boys." I smile to myself. The fact he don't already know that, only proves he has no idea how his ranch operates outside of his office. I've said all I can. Now all I can do is stand back and wait for his answer.

"Take the men you need," he sighs in defeat. "But you keep it clean," he warns with a stern look in his eyes. "I don't want any comebacks from this, and I sure as hell don't want anything ruining the wedding next Saturday."

The disapproving growl Cole makes, from behind me, diverts Pops' attention, and I prepare myself for some conflict. Cole ain't one to leave his thoughts unsaid, and he ain't taking the news that Pops is remarrying all that well. He always was Mom's favorite, and it don't matter how many years she's been gone, he ain't ever gonna accept another woman coming into our home. Especially a woman like Cora Wildman.

"I don't wanna hear any of that shit either." Pops' eyes home in on my brother. "You're all gonna make Cora and her daughter feel welcome here, they're part of this family now." The way Cole stares back at him proves he has no intention of backing down.

"Don't you worry about my shit, Pops, I'm taking it with me. I ain't sticking around here to watch that gold digger get her claws into you. I'm helping Garrett bring back the herd, then I'm out."

The news comes just as much as a shock to me, as it does my father.

"What do you mean you're out?" Pops makes that cocky laugh that gets right under my skin and when I turn around, I see my brother's determination grow even wilder as he moves closer and leans over our old man's desk.

"I warned you that I wouldn't sit back and watch you make a fool of yourself and this family. You barely know the woman, she comes from a whole different world to ours, and she's young enough to be your daughter. Women like her feast on men like you. I'm leaving Copper Ridge." He starts heading for the door, but I refuse to let him leave.

"Cole!" I step in his way and let him see how fucking mad I am.

"Let him go, son," My stubborn-assed father acts like he ain't bothered, but I pay no attention to him and shove Cole back into the wall so I can talk some sense into his head.

"You ain't going nowhere. We need ya here."

"Better get used to not having me around, Garrett, because as soon as we're back from fucking up those rustlers, I'm outta here."

I raise my fist and prepare myself to put it through his face, and Pops stands up and rushes to grab my arm.

"Don't ya remember what your mom always told you, boys? Ya raise all the hands ya want, but ya never turn 'em on each other."

"And what do you think Mom would say about you marrying a whore?" Cole stares our father right in the eye, and although I see the rage stirring inside them, I see a whole lot of sadness too. The same kinda anger radiates from our father, yet somehow, he manages to keep it contained.

"Incase you hadn't noticed, your mother ain't here, Cole. Ain't no one wishes that were different more than I do." Pops slowly releases my arm and backs down, and when a deep throated chuckle comes from behind us we all turn our heads.

My youngest brother, Wade, stands in the door frame, watching us with a smug grin on his face.

"Looks like I made it home just in time for the fireworks."

Taking off his hat, he tosses it at the table; then pushing his hand through his floppy, brown hair, he moves into hug Pops.

"Good to have you home, son." Pops wraps Wade up in his arms, and when he gives him a firm slap on his back, Wade flinches.

"I took a fall last weekend, still a little tender," he explains.

"I didn't think you'd make it." This is the first time I've seen my old man smile in a while.

"Yeah, well, those buckle bunnies will just have to make do with riding saddles this weekend. I hear there's a wedding here that needs crashing," Wade seems supportive of the whole Cora situation, but that's him all over. Unlike my brother and me, he's a go-with-the-flow kinda guy. Guess he got that trait from our mother.

Cole's shoulder slams into mine as he barges past. He stops to hug Wade, then turns to Pops with a serious-as-fucking-death look on his face.

"Sorry I won't be around to watch your shit show." He marches out the door, and when Wade calls out after him to ask where he's heading, he gets nothing in response.

"That, right there, is called a quitter, boys. There's always one in the family." Pops retakes the seat at his desk and picks up a cigar.

MAISIE

"That's over ten miles now, and all I've seen is open fields." I slam my head back against the car headrest and look up at the roof.

How has my life come to this?

"That's the beauty of the place, darling. Just look at all this scenery."

"We both know the only beauty you see in this place is old man Carson's bank balance." The suggestion earns me an immediate death stare and her eyes flick towards the driver, her fiancé sent to pick us up from the airport, just to remind me we're not alone. His eyes meet mine in the rearview mirror, and when he smirks, I roll my eyes at him.

"I won't have you call him that again. Bill Carson is a very kind, handsome and well-respected man." Mom takes the compact from her purse and uses it to reapply her lipstick while I shift my body, so I can avoid her and stare out the window.

I'm in no mood to be hearing all the wonderful things about her latest victim. I can guarantee that, right now, Bill probably feels like the luckiest man on the planet. There's no denying that my mother's an attractive woman. She's fun, spirited and will go above and beyond to please. Unfortunately for Bill, this version of her only lasts until the ring is on her finger. Some learn quicker than others that all she really is, is a bottom-feeder with a touch of class.

Over the eighteen years of my life, my mom has pulled some selfish stunts, but this has to be up there with the worst of them. I had a good life in L.A., great friends, a busy social life and my mother's decided to take me away from all of that so she can marry some rich, old rancher that lives over a thousand miles away. Because of that decision I miss out on the blow-out summer with all my friends that I deserve, before I start art school in the fall.

Bill Carson will be mom's fifth husband in eight years, and as much as I'd like to think he's her end game, I know my mother is always looking to upgrade.

"We're here," she eventually taps my leg to get my attention. When the car turns, and we drive through the fancy ,wood-carved gate that reads Copper Ridge Ranch, I can't help feeling deflated by all the fun I'm gonna miss out on back home.

"At least *pretend* to be happy about this, darling," she whispers, taking in a deep breath and pasting on a smile ready for her grand arrival.

I have to admit the place looks impressive. We drive up a track that's lined with white fences, and I notice a few horse corrals and the huge out-buildings that are scattered around. Due to Mom's past conquests, I've lived in some extravagant places over the years. This place is different. It's nothing like the glamorous mansions with palm trees and backyard pools in L.A. Here it's rustic, and with all the people bustling around the yard and doing various jobs, it's a little chaotic too.

The car pulls to a stop, and when the driver gets out to open Mom's door, I climb out behind her and take in the large, luxurious cabin in front of me. I always thought cabins were supposed to be small and quaint. This one is huge, and yet it still has that homely vibe you'd expect.

There's a porch that looks as though it wraps all the way around the house, and I'm just admiring the swinging chair that hangs from it, when the front door bursts open, and a man wearing jeans, a blue shirt and a Stetson storms out onto the yard.

"Hello there." Mom immediately shows him her pearly whites, and he doesn't even give her the respect of an acknowledgement. The arrogant asshole just marches right past us, gets into a pick-up truck, and kicks up dust as he skids off.

Mother doesn't let his rudeness knock the smile from her face, and when another guy dressed almost the same steps out onto the porch, he immediately gets my attention. He looks a little older than the other one, and although he doesn't acknowledge us either, I get the impression it isn't out of arrogance. I watch him move to the far end of the porch, clutching the wood rail in his hands and making a heavy sigh that suggests he's got something on his mind, as he looks out at the mountain range in the distance.

I can't recall ever seeing a man as handsome as he is. Maybe it's because he's different from all the boys back in L.A., who get weekly haircuts and fill their Instagram with pictures of themselves at the gym. Or maybe it's because he isn't a boy at all. What I'm looking at right here, is a man. A rugged, rough man with chiseled features that make it impossible for me to stop staring at him. I can't quite see what his hair is like because of the hat he's wearing, but I'm guessing it'll be dark, just like his overgrown stubble.

He closes his eyes and lowers his head like he's holding the weight of the world on his shoulders and, for a few short seconds, I forget how sorry I feel for myself, so I can wonder what's troubling him.

"How ya doin'?" I get distracted by the voice that comes

from the front door, and when I look toward it, I see another handsome guy step out of the house. At least this one has a welcoming smile on his face.

"Welcome to Copper Ridge," he tells us, and when Mom holds out her hand for him, he takes it and winks over the top of it before he kisses her. The giggle she makes is pathetic, and I have to look away out of embarrassment.

"Name's Wade," he introduces himself.

"Pleased to meet you, Wade. I'm Cora, and this is my daughter, Maisie."

Wade lifts his hat slightly from the front and with a dirty smirk on his lips, his eyes take their time scanning me over.

"I've heard a lot about you." Mom keeps that fake smile firmly in place. "Wade, here, is a rodeo star," she tells me, and I nod my head courteously so I at least appear interested.

"I don't know about a star, but I'm pretty hot shit," he tells me before heading for the trunk.

"I got these, Dalton." He takes the suitcases from the guy who picked us up from the airport, and dismisses him with a nod of his head.

"Ma'am," Dalton smiles at me before taking his order and heading off in the direction of one of the stables.

"Follow me ladies. Let me show you into your new home." Wade turns to lead us toward the house, and I throw Mom a scowl before we follow him.

As I make my way up the porch steps, my focus gets distracted again by the tall, handsome stranger, who still doesn't seem to have any intention of acknowledging our arrival. It pisses me off. I want his attention. I want him to look at me the way Wade just did, and I'm really curious as to what's got him so preoccupied.

I'm just about to step through the door when his head turns to look over his shoulder, and when his dark, brown eyes peer into mine, the warning they heed sets a chill over my skin.

His lips remain straight, and I take the slight nod of his head as his version of a greeting.

It's rude and unwelcoming, but I can't help being attracted to the edge of danger I sense from him. And for the first time in over a week, I smile as I follow my mom inside.

"Welcome," I assume the man, who kisses my mother when we get inside, is Bill. He isn't quite as old as I imagined him to be, and he's much more handsome than her last husband.

"You must be Maisie." He smiles, stepping forward and taking my hands in his. "I've had a room prepared for you. Your mother tells me you'll be leaving us in a few months for college, but that room is yours now. I want you to think of this ranch as your home." I sense the sincerity in his words, but it still doesn't make me want to be here.

"Wade, why don't you take Maisie and show her where her room is? She's in the guest room next to Garrett's." He speaks to his son and then turns his attention to me again.

"Freshen yourself up, unpack, explore, do whatever you want to do. We're having a family dinner tonight so make sure you're at the table for seven." He steps towards my mother, wrapping his arm around her shoulders before leading her away.

"Come on, I'll take you to your room." Wade leads me to the staircase and then up to the landing that looks down over the cozy, but spacious, living area. He tries to make polite conversation by asking me how the journey was and what I'm going to study when I start college, and I make it hard by only giving him one word answers.

He stops and opens a door for me, and when I step inside the room, I suddenly feel even further away from L.A.

The bed is made of wood, and the curtains and bedspread are made from heavy, tribal patterned fabric.

Nothing in here really matches, and yet it goes together well. The room has a warm, comforting vibe that makes it feel homely.

But this is not my home. If the years taught me anything, it's to not get too comfortable anywhere.

"You got a good view out onto the yard," Wade lifts my case onto the bed and moves to look out the window. "And in the winter months, you're gonna really appreciate that fire," he gestures his head toward the open fire that's on the other side of the room. I can't recall ever seeing a fireplace in someone's bedroom before.

"I'm not gonna be here in the winter months. I just have to get through the summer." I let out a long, heavy sigh and join him to look out the window.

"You'll be back for holidays, Thanksgiving, Christmas," he points out.

"Don't count on it." Mom is a big fan of living lavishly. She enjoys nights out in fancy restaurants and trendy cocktail bars. I can't see this one lasting very long.

The yard is busy, everyone seems to be bustling around, doing their jobs, and this is nothing like what I imagined my summer to look like.

"Bathroom's just down the hall. You can freshen up there." Wade smiles like he can sense how sad I am. I don't want his pity. I want to be back in L.A., with my friends.

"I'll see ya at dinner," nodding his head, he moves out the door, closing it behind him.

I take a shower and stay in my room until it's time to head down for dinner, like Bill requested. Bill sits at the head of the table and mother has already settled into her role as lady of the house, sitting at the opposite end with a satisfied look on her face.

Wade stands up as soon as he notices me, and he pulls out the chair beside him for me to sit down. I nod my gratitude before taking a seat, and when I realize that the handsome guy I saw on the porch earlier is sitting directly opposite me, I start to feel nervous. I can feel his eyes watching me as I pick up my napkin and lay it across my lap.

"I don't think you've been introduced to my eldest son, Maisie. This here's, Garrett, and his bite's way worse than his bark." Bill chuckles at his own joke while Garrett nods his head at me, in the same subtle way he did earlier.

"Pleased to meet you," I manage to smile, despite the fact my cheeks feel like they're on fire. Then I almost jump out of my skin when a woman comes out of nowhere. Leaning over my shoulder to place a plate in front of me. A very loaded plate that contains a slab of meat almost the size of my head.

"Maisie, this is Josie. Let her know if you have any dietary requirements, and she'll get it catered to," Bill introduces the woman, who seems much younger than most other housekeepers I've encountered. She's attractive, with mid-length, chestnut-coloured hair and a welcoming smile.

"Pleased to meet you, Miss Wildman." She bows her head to me, and I smile at her politely, trying not to be intimidated by the half a cow I've got on my plate.

"Hope you like steak," Wade nudges me with his shoulder and snorts a laugh before he picks up his knife and fork and digs into his food like he's been starved.

I pick up my cutlery and try not to look across at Garrett. Now that he isn't wearing his hat, I can see him properly; and if it's possible, he looks even more appealing.

His dark, brown hair is short at the back and sides and a little longer on top. If it wasn't pushed over to one side, it would hang over those hooded eyes of his, and I can't help wondering what that might look like.

You can tell, just from looking at Garrett, that he's a real man. He's got cuts and scrapes on his hands, and now that his shirt sleeves are rolled up I can see the veins in his forearms. It's not until Mother strikes up a conversation that I realize my attempts not to look at him have failed.

"Bill, I'm sure you told me you had three sons."

The old man glances at the empty space that's been laid at the table and clears his throat.

"Unfortunately, Cole couldn't join us tonight. He's…"

"Pissed at the fact you're marrying a woman half your age, who you've only known for three months," my mouth runs away with me, and while Wade almost chokes on his steak with amusement, Garrett appears unimpressed by my outspokenness.

"Maisie!" Mother blushes, then gives me a warning glance when she thinks no one's looking.

"No, Cora, please. Maisie is right. Cole isn't happy about the arrangement. He never did get over what happened with his mother. But he will come around. He'll have to, because nothing's changing." The way Bill stares me down almost dares me to argue, and it reveals a different side to him. Thankfully, Wade quickly makes an attempt to break the tension.

"Since you'll be spending the summer here, you're gonna need to learn how to ride, and there ain't no better teacher than me. I gotta few weeks before my next competition, if you want to be taught by the master."

"I can't see that happening." I shake my head and take a sip of my water, trying to ignore the fact that Garrett is still drilling me with his eyes, across the table.

"You *have* to learn to ride. You can't be part of this family and not know how to ride a horse," Wade laughs, and it feels awkward when the rest of the room remains silent.

"Yeah, well, I never asked to be part of this family, and I *certainly* never asked to spend my summer out here in the ass-end of nowhere. I appreciate your offer Wade, but it won't be required." When Wade drops his head to look at his plate, I feel a little guilty for snapping.

I'm fully aware of how rude I'm being, and he seems like a nice enough guy. He shouldn't have to take the brunt of my anger.

We spend the rest of the meal in silence, and as soon as Garrett's finished his last mouthful, he wipes his mouth with a napkin and stands up from the table.

"You ready, Wade?" he growls at his brother, as he picks up his hat and places it back on his head.

"Hell yeah, I'm ready!" Wherever they're going, Wade seems excited about it. He practically leaps onto his feet.

"Remember what I said." Bill gives Garrett a stern look as he heads out the dining room, closely followed by Wade, who at least has the courtesy to say goodbye.

CHAPTER 3
GARRETT

Out here, the night is black, and the silence is deadly. Grid four is the most remote section of the ranch, and the line-camp cabin we have out here is the perfect place for our talk with Trevor Henson.

When we hear a truck pull up outside, Wade puts out his cigarette and sits a little straighter in the wooden chair he's resting in. I don't know how he always manages to stay so relaxed. But then, I figure that's the privilege you get when you're the little brother of a family.

Wade left home to join the rodeo when he was eighteen, and Pops saw him off proudly. Me? I can't even spend an extra hour in town without him calling my phone and asking me where I am or telling me something's gone wrong.

The door to the cabin opens, and when Cole steps inside, I don't know how I feel about him being here.

Yeah, I'm relieved he showed up, but he's being a dick, and if he sees through on his word and ends up leaving the ranch, it'll be me that suffers it.

"Didn't think you'd be coming. You weren't at dinner," I let him know I ain't happy by the tone of my voice. Pops is marrying Cora, whether we agree with it or not. If she *is* a gold-digging whore, it should make Cole all the more determined to stick around and defend what belongs to us.

"I told you I'd help get the herd back, didn't I?" He moves across the room and rests his ass on the table beside Wade.

"Hey, at least one good thing has come out of this ridiculous marriage. The daughter ain't bad to look at, is she, Garrett?" Wade wiggles his eyebrows, as

I clench my fists and tamp down the niggle inside me.

"Ain't noticed," I lie.

Of course I fucking noticed. It's impossible not to, and I already know the girl's gonna be trouble. The boys in the bunkhouse ain't gonna be getting much work done this summer with her around, that's for sure.

"I got a look at her when I left earlier. She's pretty enough." Cole readjusts his hat and rolls up his sleeves.

"Pretty, blue eyes. Long, blonde hair and an ass as tight as...."

"Will you shut the fuck up?" I cut Wade off. I'm about to do whatever it takes to get information from Trevor, the last thing I want is the image of her in my head while I do it.

"Jeezzz, good to see nothing's changed around here. You're still as uptight as ever." Wade rolling his fucking eyes at me makes me bite.

"Yeah well, we don't all get to ride broncs and buckle bunnies for a living. Some of us have a job to do."

"A job? I got a job, Garrett. My job's to entertain and stay a-fuckin'- live!" Wade is usually hard to get a reaction from, but I'm getting one now. "Don't you dare blame me for the fact you feel trapped here." His chair falls back when he stands up, and he's looking the maddest I've seen him in a real long time.

"I ain't trapped. I'm just doing what's right. This ranch is ours, and I want something to leave behind when I'm gone."

"Leave behind, to who? When was the last time you were with a woman, one who you didn't meet in a bar, after an auction, and fuck in a motel room?" My little brother sniggers, and when I look to Cole for backup, he just shrugs. I remind myself that arguing is a pointless exercise, and instead of answering back, I cold-stare him.

"There's a life beyond this ranch, Garrett. The only person keeping you from it is you."

I ignore the fact that all he says is true. Even if I did want a woman, I can't imagine it'd be easy to find one prepared to make a life with a man who works fourteen hours a day. And if by some miracle I did, she sure as shit wouldn't accept the things I'm willing to do to protect this place.

The sound of another engine cuts through the tense silence, and when the door bursts open and Trevor Henderson tumbles through it, he's followed closely by Finn and Tate.

Tate was the first person I employed when I figured we needed to go back to the way my grandfather ran the ranch.

He's done some time in County, but I'm hardly one to judge him on that. Only difference between me and him is that I've never been caught.

Tate's got the brawn, he's got the courage, and he just needs to learn how to be smart about things.

There are plenty of good lawyers out there, but a Carson needs a dirty one.

Miles managed to get Tate a reduced sentence on his manslaughter charge, and since it's hard to find a job when you're on parole, he was happy to take the one I offered him here. So far, he's proved himself to be reliable, and he's worked hard and shown me loyalty. From my men, I ask for nothing more.

Finn's new. He came here on Mitch's recommendation. I don't know much, other than the fact he's linked to an old friend of his. He called in a favor when the kid was due for release from jail. Finn may be young, but I already see a fight in the boy that I know will be invaluable.

"Found the fucker pulling out from the Mason's ranch," Tate informs me, slamming his toecap into Trevor's ribs before lighting himself a smoke.

"Wonder what he was doing there?" Wade steps forward and starts circling the floor where he lies.

"We followed him for a few miles, then pulled him over," Tate continues.

"You shot out my back window, you asshole!" Trevor looks up at him from the floor where he's lying with his hands roped behind his back, and we hear all the air hiss from his lungs when Tate stamps on his stomach.

"Now, are you really in the position to be calling me an asshole?" He crouches down to his level, and his eyes threaten to unleash hell.

"Get him in the chair," I order Finn, who immediately does as I ask, pulling Trevor off the floor and slamming his ass into the chair that Wade's already positioned in the center of the room. I nod my head at Cole, who drags the bear trap from the corner and places it in front of him.

"What…What the fuck's that?" Trevor asks, staring down at it as if he's never seen one before.

"You've lived in these mountains long enough to know what that is," I laugh at him, as Cole pries the jaws of the contraption open, to set it.

"Yeah, but…but, what ya gonna do with it?" The sweat dripping out of his pores, and the way his eyes flick between mine and the trap that's just inches from his feet, suggests to me he knows exactly what I intend to do with it.

"That's up to you. See, I know you had something to do with the robbery that happened here last night. And for that, you're gonna be punished. How bad that punishment is will depend on how fast you tell us how we're gonna get our cattle back."

"I don't know where they are, I swear, and I didn't have anything to do with it." He shakes his head and lies to me. *Stupid fucking bastard.*

"Trevor, make this easy on yourself, and think back to that night a few months back when you saw me and Cole in Cahoots. You'd drank too much whiskey. Your mouth was running away with itself, like usual, and you were bragging about how you'd made enough money to buy that shiny, new truck of yours." If it's possible, Trevor's face turns even whiter.

"We go back a lot of years, Trevor. Your pa even wore the brand." Trevor nods his head frantically. Maybe he's relying on that fact to save him, the same way he did when we were kids.

"Do you remember back in high school, when your slut sister was flashing her pussy around like a mare in heat? How all the boys in our year fucked her for sport? Who showed you some fucking loyalty by turning her whore ass down, when she put it on a plate? Who beat the shit into Will Sommerton when he knocked her up, because her daddy had skipped town and her pussy-assed brother was too fucking weak to do anything about it?"

The pathetic piece of shit has tears rolling out of his eyes because he knows everything I'm saying is true.

"Your daddy tried screwing us, and he feared the repercussions of his actions so bad he left his whole family behind and ran. Did we ever make you suffer for it?" I question him.

Trevor's head shakes, and he fails to look me in the eye. After Grandpa died, a lot of the men who wore our brand abandoned their post. Mitch blames my father for the fact he's the only one of them left now, and he's right to. Pops never did see the value in the men who vowed their loyalty to us, men who would do whatever it took to ensure the ranch kept running and the Carson name got upheld. The branded men were a brotherhood, reprobates who formed a family of their own in the bunkhouse. Men like Tate and Finn, who were looking for a place to belong and found it here on our ranch. They weren't owned by us. The brand they wore only showed where they belonged, and who they were loyal to, and they were fucking proud of it.

Now they're extinct.

I never blamed anyone for leaving after Grandpa died. Pops made it clear to them all that the brand meant nothing to him, but there are ways of going out, and the way Roger Henson chose to make his exit proved he never had any real loyalty to our family.

I'd bet the fact he's never come back to town ain't out of fear. How can you be fearful when you're dead? And knowing how seriously Mitch takes the promise he made my grandpa as a boy, that'd be my guess as to where Roger is.

"I guess we should have judged you on your old man's actions, after all. Turns out you're the same kinda dishonest cunt he was."

Trevor closes his eyes and takes a deep breath when he realizes there ain't nothing that's gonna get him out of the shit he's in.

"I told 'em the easiest route in and out," he mumbles feebly. "But I wasn't with 'em, I swear. I even got an alibi to prove it." He looks up at me with eyes begging for mercy, and I decide that I'll show him a little.

"Arm or leg?" I ask, calmly watching the horror spread on his face.

"Wait… I do know where you can find them! They'll be heading for the border! There's a stop-off point near Great Falls. If you leave now, you can get to them before they pass. I can give you the exact location." It's the voice of a desperate man that we're hearing, and I turn to Tate to give him his order.

"Head to the bunkhouse. I want Seth, Otis, Derrick, and two cattle lorries ready to leave straight away."

"Gotcha, boss," he tips his head at me, and when Finn automatically goes to leave with him, I call him back.

"You wait here. I got a different job for you."

"Speak," my attention immediately goes back to Trevor.

"There's a small ranch three miles west of the entrance to the 15. That's where you'll find 'em," He's got a fearful quiver in his voice, but he starts to look more relaxed as I take in what he tells me, and nod my head.

"Arm or leg?" I ask again when he's finished, knowing that that relief of his is about to be short-lived.

"I told you where they are. You can't…"

I move closer to the worthless piece of shit and throw my fist at his jaw to shut him up.

"I told you you'd be punished for fucking with me. The fact you just told me how to rectify it earned you your choice. Arm or fucking leg?" I repeat myself, losing my fucking patience and desperate to get on the road.

"Arm." Trevor closes his eyes, knowing it's a pointless fight.

"Untie him," I nod my head at Wade, who gets straight to work, and when Trevor starts to struggle Cole helps wrestle him to the floor, then rests his knees on the back of his legs and uses his knife to cut through the rope. When he's done, Wade helps pin him down while Cole stretches out Trevor's right arm.

"Wait, wait… that's my roping arm. Do the left." He looks up at me, pleading with his eyes and sounding pathetic.

"Nah," I shake my head and smile wickedly. "Your daddy was a rustler, you fix for the rustlers, and although I doubt you could ride a pony through a parade, I'd rather not take my chances." I shove his face into the floor with my boot, and nod to Cole, who stretches Trevor's arm out as far as it will reach between the jaws. Then, making sure he's well clear himself, he forces it down to set off the spring release.

The sound of Trevor's bones crunching and the agonized

scream that comes from his throat fill the cabin, and I release his head so I can see the pain on his face, too.

I wait until those screams turn into moans. It's important that he hears me give Finn his next instruction.

"You'll find another trap in that cupboard over there. I'll call you when we get to the location. If he's telling the truth, you can release him and drop him off at the hospital."

"And if he ain't?" Finn asks, with a snigger.

"Then you get that trap out the cupboard, set it on his leg and wait until I get back."

I wait for Finn to nod and let me know he understands, before I slap Wade on the chest. "Let's go get our herd back." I head for the door, and when I open it I'm not at all surprised to see Mitch waiting outside.

The old man's been working the bunkhouse since he was a boy, and he may not be a Carson by blood, but he picks up the same respect as one from anyone who works here.

"Pops send ya?" I check, lighting up a smoke and looking up at the stars. It's a clear night, and the sky is full of 'em.

"Nah, I rode out with Tate and Finn to pick him up. Figured when you sent 'em, something was gonna go down, and I didn't wanna miss out."

I laugh at the old man. He'll never change, and I'm glad for it as I've learnt more from him than my father ever cared to teach me.

"I know where the herd is. We're setting out now, if you wanna come?" I offer. Mitch may not be as young as he used to be, but he's as handy as any man I got.

Rustlers are ruthless men; it never hurts to have experience on your side.

"I heard," he chuckles to himself, and it tugs at my curiosity.

"Whatcha finding so funny?" I stare back at him.

"You just remind me of your Uncle Jimmer, is all," he lights up a smoke of his own.

Pops would hate to hear him say that. It's been a long time since my dad spoke to his brother. They fell out years ago after he left the ranch and decided to become an outlaw. I can't remember him, I was only two years old when he left Montana, and he's never cared to visit since. I figure he wouldn't get a warm welcome from Pops anyway. He never did forgive him for bailing on our family, and I hope I'll be able to find the strength to do better if Cole sees through on his word.

"That a good or bad thing?" I ask,

"For the ranch, it's a great thing. For folk like Trevor, in there, not so much," Mitch sniggers

"You go get your cattle back, son. I'll stay here with the young 'un. And Garrett..." When I turn back to look at him, I know exactly what he's gonna say.

"Whatever it takes." I finish his sentence before he can. And watch the smile crack on his face.

"Whatever it takes." He pulls his hat lower to cover his eyes, before heading inside the cabin.

The loud sounds of whoops and yells disturb me, and when I open my eyes, I sigh in depression when I remember where I am.

Reaching over to the night stand I lift up my phone and realize it's only 8am, and after dragging my ass out of bed, I look out the window onto the yard and see it's already busy.

Wade's putting on a show for all the cowboys in the huge corral that's closest to the house. He's got a smart grin on his face as he holds on tight to the front of his saddle, and gets thrown around by a horse that looks like it doesn't want to be ridden.

His audience sit on the fence surrounding him, cheering him on and laughing with each other. It's far too early for this much enthusiasm, but figuring I don't stand a chance of getting back to sleep, I head down to the kitchen to grab a coffee.

The house seems empty, which suits me fine. I'd much rather wallow in my misery alone. There is however, coffee in the pot, so I navigate around the cupboards to try and find a mug to put it in.

"Top left," the deep, husky voice that comes from behind me has me spinning around, and when I see Garrett standing in the doorway, wearing blue jeans and a tight gray shirt, I have to convince my eyes not to stare at his solid chest.

"Sorry?" He's so good to look at that I realize I completely missed what he just said.

"I figured you were looking for a mug for that coffee?" his eyes drop to the pot I'm holding in my hand.

"If you are, you'll find one in the top left cupboard."

He moves forward and stretches his arm up over my head, and when that chest I'm trying not to look at is suddenly right in my face, all I can think about is reaching my hands up and seeing if it feels as solid as it looks.

"You missed breakfast." He places the mug on the counter before leaning back and resting his ass against the basin.

"How did I miss breakfast? It's only just after eight?" I laugh, turning my back to him so I can take a breath as I pour my coffee, then head to the refrigerator to find some cream.

"Half the day's gone by eight," he points out, and when I slam the refrigerator door shut, I notice the few extra scrapes on his hands and the bruise on his left cheek. I decide not to mention them as I don't want him to think I'm paying attention.

"So, what is there to do around here?" I add the cream to my coffee, and when I start searching for a spoon, he's already holding one out for me.

"Plenty, if you don't mind hard work." He watches me stir, like he's critiquing my every move and it should piss me off, but it doesn't. If anything, I kinda like it.

"Well, I'm not here to work. In fact, if I had my way, I wouldn't be here at all."

"You couldn't have made that any clearer if you tried." When his eyes narrow and his brow scrunches together, I feel my insides clench. "But I'll give you a heads up for while ya here."

He steps even closer to me, resting his hands on the counter either side of my hips and caging me in.

"Be fucking nice." The hint of threat in his whisper makes my skin shiver.

"And if I'm not?" I stare up into his cold, dark eyes with the intention to prove I'm not afraid of him, but I forget all that when I notice the tiny fleck of green in them.

"Then this will be the longest summer of your fucking life."

He shoves himself off the counter and heads back out the door, and I wait until I hear the front door slam before I allow myself to breathe again.

Since I missed breakfast, I decide to make my own, and after locating a bowl, I put together a fruit salad and sit up at the breakfast bar to eat it.

"Mornin'," Wade steps in a few minutes later, covered in dust, taking off his hat and pulls his hand through his hair.

"Morning yourself." I roll my eyes, wondering how the hell I'm gonna manage an entire summer in this place.

"Take it you ain't a mornin' person?" he chuckles as he heads for the coffee machine, and after realizing it's empty, he takes a water from the fridge instead.

I don't answer his question, just keep on eating.

"The folks went into town to meet with the wedding organizer." He continues to make an effort with me, and I give him nothing back. All I can think about is all the fun Annie and Jeorgie will be having without me.

"Jeez, you got your period or are you always this happy?" Wade shakes his head as he laughs, and I drop my spoon into my bowl and stare at him viciously.

"My whole life's been disrupted for this stupid, fucking marriage, so forgive me for being a little pissed off with life right now."

Wade seems unaffected by my outburst, and when he smiles, it irritates the hell out of me.

"I get that, and these hills feel a million miles from the ones in L.A. But for now, they're all you got to look at. Drop the attitude, and who knows? You might even find yourself having some fun."

When I notice his split lip and the slight swelling of his right eye, I study him more curiously.

"Did you get into a fight?" I ask, because questioning Wade seems so much easier than it would Garrett. With him, I can barely get any words out at all.

"Summat like that," he smiles, picking up an apple from the bowl and tossing it in his hand before he heads back out, and leaves me alone.

It's just past midday before my boredom level reaches its peak. I've explored the house. I've tried watching the shit they put on the tv during the day, and none of my friends are answering their phones, which I'm guessing is because they're busy enjoying summer. And as much as it pains me, I finally admit to defeat and drag myself off the couch to go and locate Wade.

Taking a quick glance around the yard, I see plenty of cowboys, but I don't see him. The tall, stocky guy, who's shifting hay from the back of a truck into one of the barns, stops to lift his hat to me, and I fake him a smile before moving on to check the stables.

I've never actually been in a stable before, and I'm surprised that I find the smell in here almost inviting. There are eight stalls altogether, and I'm immediately drawn to the black stallion, whose head is hanging over the stall door to my left.

He carries an obnoxious presence, but he's beautiful, and I decide that if I'm gonna touch him, I'm better off approaching him with confidence.

My fingers shake a little as I hold them out to him, and just before I touch his snout, he shakes his head and makes a loud *brrrrrr* that has me leaping backward.

I don't even have to turn around to figure out that the smug laugh coming from behind me belongs to Wade.

"That's Thunder, he's Garrett's horse," Wade steps up beside me and raises his arm to tap the horse's thick, muscular neck.

"Figured the arrogant bastard would belong to him," I smirk, as I stroke my fingers through his mane. Wade must agree with my analysis because he laughs.

"So, did you come out here just to look, or do you wanna have some real fun?" He dares me, and I figure I should at least give his idea of *fun* a shot....

Ten minutes later, I'm walking out towards the corral with Wade, leading the fully-saddled horse that I'm apparently going to ride.

"This isn't the same one you were riding this morning, is it?" I double-check, nervously.

"No, darlin'. This one's broken,"

"You're giving me a broken one?" I stare back at him in horror, and the way he shakes his head and huffs a laugh at me, irritates me.

"Broken *in*, it means she's tame," he strokes at her brown and white nose. "I broke her in myself, so I know she's a safe bet. Jump up, Princess." He stops when we get to the center, and when he taps the saddle, I look around me expectantly.

"You want me to just jump on?" Now it's my turn to laugh. There's no way I'm getting on this horse, unaided.

"Here. This is a stirrup," he grabs the part hanging off the saddle, that I assume I've got to put my foot into, "put your left foot in, grip here…" he takes my hand and forces it on the front part of the saddle to demonstrate, "…and then swing yourself on." He explains like it's a simple task.

"There's no way I'm getting up there!" The horse's back is level with my chin. It's impossible.

"C'mon, I'll give ya a foot up." Wade helps me get my foot in the stirrup, and without any warning, he pushes under my ass and lands me on the saddle.

"That was not a foot up. *That* was an excuse to touch my ass." I glare down at him as I try to find myself a more comfortable position.

"No.1, get your head out the gutter, we're practically brother and sister, and no. 2, Wade Carson never makes excuses." He keeps the cocky grin on his face as he makes some adjustments to those stirrup things, and I grip hold of the reins, taking some calming breaths to prepare myself.

"Now, Gem here knows what she's doing, so let her lead you while you find your balance. I got her, so she's not going anywhere." He shows me the long rope in his hand that's attached to her head piece.

"Okay." I nod, trying to show some confidence, and when Wade makes a clicking sound, I grip the saddle a little tighter when the horse starts to move.

"Relax your body, loosen your hips and let yourself move with her," he instructs, and I follow.

"Now, hold the reins in your left hand and tug gently." When I do as he says, the horse immediately stops.

"Good start..." Wade flashes me that wide grin, and it feels kinda good that I got it right. "Now to tell her to move on, squeeze her belly with your calves and give her the command,"

I tense my legs and try to replicate the noise Wade made to get her going, and to my surprise, I pull it off, and she starts walking again.

"Like that?" I feel the smile lift my cheeks. I can't help feeling a little proud of myself, and although riding a horse isn't something that I've ever had on my bucket list, I think it's kinda cool.

"It's a start," Wade steps further away, giving us more rope, and I continue to ride in a slow circle around him. Eventually, he makes that circle even wider, and my confidence continues to grow as my body starts to fall in sync with the horse's movements.

"You wanna go faster?" Wade asks, and as I nod enthusiastically, the thrill swells in my stomach.

"Ok, it's gonna feel a little different, but just keep doing what you're doing and let your body follow hers. If you feel yourself going off balance, keep the reins in your hands, but grip the front of your saddle.

"This bit?" I take hold of the thing sticking up between my legs.

"That's the one. Now do exactly what you did to get her walking, and she'll know what to do."

I squeeze my legs a little tighter and click her on, and she immediately changes pace. Wade's, right, it does feel different, and when I feel myself slipping slightly on the saddle, I hold myself firm and try to adapt to the new rhythm.

"That's good. Keep going. We might make a cowgirl out of you yet…" he teases, and I snigger at him as I continue to do laps of the corral. I didn't expect it, and I sure don't want to admit it, but I'm actually starting to enjoy myself.

I catch a glimpse of Garrett out of the corner of my eye, he's resting his arms on the fence and watching me with that usual judgemental stare of his. I pretend not to see him, straightening my back and holding my head a little higher. I won't be intimidated by him, not one bit. At least, that's what I tell myself.

"Now you're just showing off." I blush when Wade totally calls me out, and after making a subtle glance over my shoulder to where Garrett was standing, I realize he's gone, and I can't help feeling a little disappointed.

CHAPTER 5
GARRETT

Turns out Cora Wildman has expensive taste. I dread to think how much money's been spent on this stupid, fucking wedding.

The ranch is barely recognisable; there are white and pink bows tied to anything standing, and half of Fork River has turned out to watch my father make a fool of himself.

He's only known the mysterious woman from L.A., who's 20 years younger than him, for a few months. They met online, and during the few weekends they've spent away together, she seems to have fucked all the sense right out if his head.

The folk of Fork River like to talk, and our family has always been subject to their conspiracies. Anything we do, big or small, tends to provoke interest and this wedding is no exception.

I stand beside my old man as he says his vows and try my best not to be distracted by her.

There's no denying Maisie's looking pretty in the floaty, pink bridesmaid dress she's wearing. Her long, wavy, blonde hair hangs over one shoulder, and I swear the girl has no idea how fucking beautiful she is. I've heard the way the boys in the bunkhouse talk about her, and I can't understand why it makes me want to throat-punch every single one of 'em for it.

I also can't figure why I feel an undeniable jealousy everytime I see her laughing and having fun with Wade.

I don't even know this girl, and all I've witnessed from her so far has been rude and obnoxious behavior. She's a brat. No doubt used to getting her way because her momma's too busy conjuring men like my father to keep them in champagne and fancy clothes.

I figure the sooner she leaves to go to college, the better.

After the ceremony is done, everyone spreads out onto the elaborately, decorated lawn. The town folk gather in small groups to gossip while the men, my father invited here out of obligation, network. I do my bit, making nice, and participating in their egotistical bullshit, because you never know when you might need a favor.

Cole proves he's every bit as stubborn as I expected by not showing, and although Pops hasn't said anything, I can see he's upset by it. Luckily, Wade more than makes up for our brother's absence. He's a local hero, and I can tell from the look on his face that he's lapping up all the attention he's getting from the large crowd gathered around, listening to his stories.

I'm surprised Maisie ain't there listening and swooning over him, too. In fact, there doesn't seem to be any sign of her at all.

I *should* carry on networking—Harry Denby, the livestock commissioner, is talking to the Mayor, and I should really be listening in to figure out if they have any suspicions on what happened when I took our herd back last week. But the longer I go without seeing her, the more that niggle she puts inside me spreads. So, downing the last of my champagne, I admit defeat and go in search of her.

I check the house first, but the only people there are the caterers, and after passing through the yard and having no luck, I decide to check the stables.

My feet pull to a halt when I find her, still wearing that pretty dress, as she strokes Darcy's long, white nose. She doesn't seem to know I'm here, and I prefer it that way. Watching Maisie Wildman from a distance has quickly become my guilty pleasure. It's wrong of me to let the thoughts I have in my head fester. She's far too young, and despite what she thinks, she's far too innocent. But today, I'm getting a different vibe from her.

Today, she seems sad.

Since Maisie arrived here, she's been putting on a front, and as much as I hate to find beauty in her pain, seeing her stripped back, and showing real emotion is breathtaking.

I don't want to disturb her, so I stand in silence and admire her. I lose track of how many minutes pass, and for the first time since I set my eyes on her, I make no attempts to block those thoughts from my mind. I allow myself to appreciate her, I let the idea of touching her feed my imagination, and when her big, blue eyes finally look up and fix on mine, desperation sinks into the pit of my stomach like a lead weight.

"She's a beauty, ain't she?" I gesture my head toward Darcy as I step towards her and pat the horse's neck. She's a good horse, one of the best we got here, but I struggle to look at her these days.

"She's gorgeous. I haven't seen her out, though. Is she not broken?" Maisie asks, with a much softer, sweeter voice than I'm used to hearing from her. There's no trace of that attitude she arrived here with.

"Yeah, she's broken. She was my sister's horse." A lump wedges in my throat.

"I didn't know you have a sister?" I watch the confusion scrunch up her forehead and prepare myself to say the words.

"*Had*," I swallow hard and try not to let the pain consume me.

"I'm sorry." Maisies eyelashes flutter, and her cheeks flush pink, proving that even pity looks pretty on her.

I know how to appreciate beauty. I live and work among it everyday. It's there every morning when I open the door, stretched out for miles in front of me.

But this is different. This is the kinda beauty that hurts. It's desperate and it makes me feel selfish because I want to hide it from the world and keep it all to myself.

"She loved this horse, and this horse loved her." I explain, continuing to show Darcy the affection she's been lacking lately. No one around here ever talks about Bree anymore, and I'm the worst culprit for it. But for some reason standing here like this, I feel the urge to speak about her.

"What was her name? I haven't seen any photographs around the house." Maisie tilts her head curiously.

"Her name was Breanna, and I figure looking at her hurts Pops too much. There used to be photos, loads of 'em. She was a great rider. You couldn't walk into a room without seeing a picture of her or a rosette she'd won. I came home from a cattle drive one day, and everything was gone. All traces of her vanished, and I never questioned Pops on it. Carson men ain't great at talkin'," I admit, focusing on brushing my fingers through Darcy's long, white mane to avoid eye contact.

"Breanna, it's a pretty name." The girl smiles awkwardly back at me, and I hate that she feels sorry for me. I ain't the person she should be feeling for.

"Who takes care of her now?" She focuses those sad eyes on the horse, and the tiny hint of a tear I see in them proves she has some empathy.

"The staff, mainly Dalton. It's been a while since she's been ridden, though… not since we lost her." My voice comes out raspy, and I have to frown to keep my own tears under control.

"That's really sad." When Maisie's eyes connect with mine, I feel them tug at something inside me. I'm not sure what it is, but I've never felt it before and, now I know it's there, I gotta feelin' things won't ever go back to the way they were.

"There you are. I've been looking all over for ya!" Wade interrupts the stare-off we're having. "They're starting the speeches, and guess who's first up?" he raises his eyebrows.

"Let me guess, the new Mrs. Carson." Maisie sighs, quickly pulling herself back together. She pastes on a smile, and rolls her eyes at my brother. "It's become her thing. I wonder if she'll reuse the one from her last wedding."

Wade laughs with her, and I can't help smirking too. It lightens the mood, and when my brother wraps his arm around her shoulder and starts leading her out of the stable, I realize his disruption couldn't have come at a better time.

I don't know what fucked-up thoughts are going through my head right now, but I have to leave 'em right here in this fucking stable. The girl's not for me. She's too naïve, despite thinking she knows the world. Whatever I'm feeling for her has to stop because there will be no good in it.

I feel the ache in the reality of that when she looks back over her shoulder at me; that sad look is back in her eyes, only this time, I sense that it's out of concern for me. I try, and recall the last time I had that, and I can't.

I nod my head at her to let her know I'm ok, and when she gives me a half-satisfied smile back, and I feel that tug inside me again, I know I'm in some real fucking trouble.

CHAPTER 6

MAISIE

"I didn't know you had a sister." I bring the subject up with Wade when I'm trotting around the corral. I'm getting quite good at this riding thing. Well, that's what he tells me anyway.

"Yeah, we had a sister," his lips raise into a sad smile.

I've been thinking about what might have happened to her, all night. Garrett opening up enough to tell me about her yesterday, felt like a step in the right direction. I just don't know what that direction leads to.

"What happened to her?" I keep my eyes focused ahead of me and continue to move with the horse, like I've been taught. I'm not good at handling awkward conversations, but I figure Wade is the easiest person to get information from.

"She died about two years ago, and it broke all our hearts." I can tell from his tone, and the stone-cold look on his face, that he doesn't want to talk about it.

"Was she sick?" I push for more. No one ever got anything from giving up easily, and I can't spend another sleepless night wondering. If I'm supposed to be part of this family, I should at least know it's history.

"No, at least I don't think she was… You're holding yourself too rigid, slacken your hips," he makes an attempt to distract me.

"Then how did she die?" I'm even more curious now. Something tells me I haven't even scratched the surface with these people.

I tug on my reins to bring Gem to a halt, and wait for his answer.

"She just fucking died, okay? She's gone." Wade snaps, and when he nears me and takes the horse's bridle in his hand, I manage to slide myself off the saddle and back onto the ground. Standing beside him, I stroke Gem's nose and curse myself for being insensitive. Seems my need for answers holds no boundaries.

"Sorry. I was insensitive. But anytime you want to talk about her…I'll always listen." I surprise myself when I realize how genuine my words are. Wade's always so upbeat, and he's been friendly and kind to me since I arrived. I hate seeing him sad.

"Around here, we like to solve problems. I guess Breanna was just another one we couldn't." He storms off, leading Gem toward the stable, and leaves me standing in the center of the corral feeling pretty fucking awful.

The house seems so big when there's no one around. Bill and Mom left this morning for their honeymoon, and I figure Wade and Garrett must be busy working on the ranch. Eating dinner at the huge table by myself was no fun, and I've just got myself settled with a book, preparing myself for an equally, lonely night when Wade comes in. He joins me in the living room, lying out on the couch opposite me and kicking up his feet. I figure the mood I put him in earlier has lifted when he smiles.

"You look bored as shit," he points out.

"That's because I *am* bored as shit." I close the book I'm reading and sigh.

"You wanna go drinking?" I like the mischievous grin on his face, it's impossible not to be tempted by it.

"I think you're forgetting that I'm only eighteen," I remind him.

"Trust me darlin', where we're going, no one's gonna care."

"Then give me ten minutes." With a sudden burst of excitement, I toss my book to one side and rush upstairs to get ready.

It takes me more like twenty minutes, than ten, to make myself look semi-presentable and when I come back down the stairs, I'm surprised to find Garrett standing beside his brother with an unimpressed look on his face. I have no idea how he manages to make angry look hot.

"Took ya time," Wade laughs, pulling his hat off the hook by the door and placing it on his head.

Garrett's already wearing his, and his dark eyes peer into mine from beneath the rim.

"This is a bad fucking idea," he growls, shaking his head with disapproval, before heading out the door. Wade shrugs his shoulders, trying to bite the awkward smile off his lips as he follows after him. Once I'm outside, Wade makes an overly theatrical deal of opening the passenger door for me, and when I hop in and climb across the bench seat Garrett is already in the driver's seat.

I spend the whole journey into Fork River wedged between the pair of them, trying not to stare at the way Garrett drives. How is it possible that the grumpy asshole can make something as simple as driving look sexy?

Fork Rivier is an odd town. It's surrounded by miles and miles of barren, open fields and a good forty-minute drive from Copper Ridge, yet, when we arrive at the quaint little town, the bar called Cahoots that Garrett parks up in front of is full of life.

Garrett marches straight inside, and as we follow him in, I notice the Carson's brand is burned into the beam above the door and make a mental note to ask Wade why, when we're alone. It's a neon light, country music, dead things on the wall kind of joint, and the barroom seems to freeze when we step inside. All eyes in the room fall upon us, and Garrett seems oblivious to it all as he makes his way toward the bar.

Wade takes the opposite approach. He pushes up the front of his hat and greets everyone who's looking. I can't figure out if he's being friendly or sarcastic.

"Why is everyone staring?" I talk under my breath, as he guides me toward the bar to join Garrett.

"Small town shit, darlin'," is the cryptic response he gives me.

I spot three guys sitting in a booth over the corner of the room, who look around Wade's age, maybe a little younger, but they seem out of place here. There ain't a cowboy hat or spur between them, and they don't look like they came here to have a good time. All three of them have serious looks on their faces and reek of danger. Garrett nods his head at the one sitting in the middle, who blows the cigarette smoke out of his lips, before subtly tipping his chin back in response.

"Since when was it ok to smoke in bars? And who are those guys?" I give in to curiosity, and ask Wade.

"Trouble." Garrett surprises me when he intercepts his brother to answer my question.

"Well, that's not technically true. They're only trouble if you get on the wrong side of 'em," Wade explains, nodding a greeting of his own over toward them.

"In this town, you're on the wrong side of everybody," Garrett points out, ignoring the no-smoking sign on the pillar right behind him when he places a cigarette between his lips and lights it up. Before I can ask him what he means by that, Wade speaks up.

"You wanna play pool?" He takes the drink Garrett just ordered him and downs it in one swallow, then slamming it on the bar, he starts making his way over toward the pool table.

"Pool sounds like fun." I pick up the full shot glass beside it, figuring it must be for me and make sure I stare Garrett right in the eyes, as I knock it back. I try my best not to choke on the afterburn, before heading over to join Wade, and I can't help finding satisfaction in the fact that Garrett's still watching when I throw him a slightly seductive look over my shoulder.

Turns out I'm surprisingly good at pool. Me and Wade play doubles and kick the ass out of two guys who work at a ranch on the other side of town. While Garrett sits at the bar by himself, staring into his drink.

When me and Wade win for the second time, the redhead who's spent over an hour eye-fucking him from over by the jukebox finally makes her way over, and blocks him from going to the bar to get us another drink. They seem familiar with each other, and watching the way he wraps his arm around her so confidently makes me wonder what it would feel like to have Garrett touch me like that. It's a hard vision to make. I can't imagine Garrett being all that free with his affection.

"You wanna go one on one?" One of the wranglers we've been playing with interrupts me from my thoughts, and when I notice his buddy has left him to go to the bar, I figure another game would be more entertaining than trying to make conversation with Garrett.

The cowboy's handsome, if you like a pretty boy. But I've learned just lately that I much prefer the mature, solitary type, and when my eyes flick back toward the bar to Garrett, I catch him watching me from under the rim of his hat again.

"Rack 'em up," I turn back around and face my opponent. I've potted a few balls before the guy starts to get handsy. At first, it's subtle and could easily be passed off as accidental, but when I lean across the table to try and take an awkward shot, and he cups my ass, I decide it's time to give him a warning.

I turn around, ready to confront him, but the words get stuck in my mouth, and my eyes stretch open when I see Garrett storming across the barroom floor, looking murderous.

The guy has no idea he's coming, and Garrett grabs him by his collar, spins him around and offers no warning before he slams his fist hard into his face. I gasp at the blood that sprays from his mouth as he falls to the floor, and when Garrett reaches down to drag the guy back onto his feet, I realize this isn't over.

Wade stands and watches with an amused look on his face and when one of the three guys, I noticed sitting in the corner earlier, goes to step in, Wade holds up his arm and shakes his head.

Garrett forces the guy, face-first, into one of the beams and I'm surprised that none of his buddies are stepping in to help him.

"I'm sorry… sorry," I hear him mumble, but Garrett doesn't let up, just holds him firm, with that furious scowl still on his face.

"Apologize to her," grabbing a fist full of the guy's hair, he pulls him away from the beam and turns him to face me. I cover my mouth with my hand when I see the state of his face.

"I'm sorry…" he somehow manages to speak, then drops his eyes to the floor like a disgraced child.

"Touch her again, and I'll fuck up more than your face," Garrett speaks a warning directly in the guy's ear before throwing him forward at the floor.

"I told you it was a bad idea," he utters under his breath to Wade on his way out the door, and when Wade blows out a breath and raises his eyebrows at me, we both follow him out.

CHAPTER 7

GARRETT

Fuck the Mason's and their disrespectful bunkhouse boys. The men we hire may not be saints, and yeah, some of 'em have done time, but at least the boys in my bunkhouse have respect.

"Jesus, Garrett, I was getting somewhere with that red piece," Wade moans as we head back to the ranch. I'm still seething, and what makes it worse is the fact I'm sure I've scared the girl. I just unleashed a little of the demon that lurks inside me, and she got a front seat at the show.

I don't respond to Wade. He'll get over it. It's only a few more days until he's back on the road, fucking whatever throws itself at him. What bothers me is that Maisie remains silent. I feel her eyes everytime they glance at me, and I hate that she's probably feeling sorry for the cocky, little prick who thought he could put his hands on her. Coming out tonight was a bad idea, and bringing her with us was an even worse one. I blame Wade for that.

We arrive back at the ranch, and Wade heads over to the

bunkhouse, hoping to carry on the party. I go straight inside the house and aim for the liquor cabinet.

The place is quiet and deserted, and after I've poured myself a whiskey, I turn around and find Maisie standing awkwardly in the middle of the room.

I don't know what she wants from me, an explanation, an apology? Either way, I ain't got one for her.

"What are you looking at?" I grasp the crystal in my hand so tight it feels like it could shatter under the pressure.

"I… I'm sorry," her bottom lip wobbles like she's gonna cry, and I wanna scrub that vulnerable, sad little look off her face when it replaces all my anger with guilt.

I don't fucking let her know that, though. The last thing I need right now is to show any weakness.

"What the fuck are you sorry for? He was the one who grabbed your ass." I swallow my drink and pour myself another straight after. I shouldn't feel this way. I shouldn't care if the girl gets felt up in a fucking bar, but I do; and realizing how much I've overreacted, for someone who supposedly doesn't give a shit, makes me furious at myself.

"I should have been clearer. He'd been pushing his luck through the game, and I… I thought it was a misunderstanding."

"Misunderstanding?" I shake my head at her in confusion.

"Yeah, I don't have a lot of experience in these kinds of things. I don't…"

"Stop." I cut her off before she overshares, and suddenly all I can think about is the fact this girl standing in front of me could, quite possibly, be a fucking virgin. I like that idea far too much to get confirmation of it.

"I'm sorry." She says those words again, and it only escalates my rage.

"Will you *stop* fucking apologizing!" I snap at her for a second time, and damn, don't it make me feel like shit when she drops her head and looks at the floor. I'm not good at this crap. Horses and herds are so much simpler to understand.

Where's the girl who came here last week, saying inappropriate things at the dinner table and being obnoxiously rude?

"I should go to bed," she sighs, and when she starts walking towards me, I suddenly feel nervous. She gets close enough to stretch up on to her tip toes and press a kiss against my stubbly jaw. I have to wonder if this girl's a liar because the way she lingers for a few seconds more than she should, and the tiny little breath she lets out into my ear, has my cock stiffening and my conscience doubting her lack of fucking experience.

"Goodnight, Garrett. Thanks for taking care of me." She's smiling when she pulls away, and I watch her all the way up the stairs and across the open landing, until she disappears into the room next to mine.

I like how that sounds… me taking care of her… and despite the shield she's had up since she arrived and her bratty little attitude, I decide it's exactly what I wanna do for the rest of the time she's here.

"Holy shit," my brother's voice takes my attention away from her door, and I glare over to where he's standing in the archway with a shit-eating grin on his face.

"Holy shit, what?" I pour him a drink and leave it on the bar, taking mine with me to rest in the high-backed leather chair beside the fire.

"You got it bad for her. I questioned it when you lost your shit with that little asshole at the bar, but that look you got on your face right now…" he shakes his finger at me and laughs. "You're fucked."

"You're talking crazy, Wade." I shake my head and knock back my whiskey.

"Nah, I know what I'm talking about." grabbing his glass and the bottle, he brings it over and tops me up before refilling his own. "I've known you my whole life, and I ain't ever seen you look at a girl like that before."

"Will you keep your damn voice down?" I whisper-yell at him, fearing she might hear.

"What's the issue? I mean, she ain't blood or nothin'," he laughs.

"No she ain't, but she's eighteen, and I'm thirty-two," I point out.

"So what? You follow in the old man's footsteps. I can think of worse scenarios." He toasts his glass and raises his shoulders at me.

"It's not what you think. And don't make out you ain't falling for it, too. I've seen you. You enjoy her company. It feels good to have her here because... because we miss Breanna." I say her name for the second time this week, and the playful smile immediately slips off Wade's lips.

"I'm fed up with acting like she never existed. I'm tired of trying to stop thinking about her. It hurts too much. This place ain't the same. Pops ain't the same. And *we* ain't the fucking same." I open up to my little brother, and he nods his head sorrowfully in agreement.

"She's just a fix, Wade. It's dangerous to let ourselves get too distant from how things were before she came. When summer's over, she'll be leaving, and everything will go back to how it was." I finish what's in my glass, then placing it on the table I stand up and squeeze my brother's shoulder as I pass him on my way to the stairs.

"Do you hate her for what she did?" he calls after me, and when I turn around, I see my carefree, crazy-assed brother's eyes brimming with tears.

"No more than I hate myself," I give him his answer ,before heading up the stairs to try and get some sleep.

CHAPTER 8
MAISIE

"Come on, girl, get ya leg over. I don't wanna be touching that ass. D'ya see what happened to the last guy who did that?" Wade makes me laugh, as I hook my foot into the stirrup and go to pull myself up.

A loud whistle sounds out across the yard, and when I look over I see Garrett coming out of the stable leading that huge, black horse of his, along with the pretty, white one that he told me belonged to his sister.

"Well, I never…" Wade utters under his breath, and when I look at him, the shock on his face has me questioning what's going on here.

"You ain't riding her today," Garrett leads the horses over to the corral entrance, where we're stood. "And you ain't riding in there either."

"But I…"

"You're riding *her* and you're riding out there, with me," he gestures his head towards the open pastures that surround the ranch, and I notice Wade's mouth drop open another inch.

"I… um,"

"Come on," Wade encourages me toward Garrett, who shocks me even more when he reaches out for my hand and guides me towards the saddle on Breanna's horse.

He doesn't even give me a chance to get my foot in the stirrup, before he places his hands on my hips and raises me with those strong arms to place me on her back.

I take the reins and grip the front the way Wade's taught me and manage to maneuver myself so I'm sitting correctly.

Garrett keeps hold of the rope that's attached to my horse and actually smiles at me before he makes hopping up onto his own saddle look effortless.

"Where you going?" I can't decide if Wade is confused or angry, as he watches Garrett double-check the clip that keeps the rope he's holding connected to my horse.

"Gotta make sure you don't get away from me." He ignores Wade's question and winks at me, and I do a terrible job of hiding the shock from my face. I'd never have guessed the man had a sense of humor.

Garrett does his own version of the clicking noise that Wade makes to get the horses moving and makes it sound sexy as hell. Despite knowing what's coming, I still startle when both horses start to move.

"We're doing a perimeter check," he calls back over his shoulder to answer his brother's earlier question, and then builds us up to a steady trot, leading us out the paddock and into the open fields

He doesn't talk to me as we ride, and oddly it doesn't feel awkward. In fact it gives me the chance to appreciate the scenery. I've been too busy stropping about being here, to actually notice how beautiful it is. The ranch is locked away by mountains, and in front of us there's a huge slope decorated with beautifully coloured trees. It dips into a long, narrow valley where the river runs through.

"That's Copper Ridge, the ranch is named after it," Garrett explains, when he notices me admiring it.

"It's pretty." I can't take my eyes off it. The way the sun lights up the different colored leaves on the trees and the sparkles on the water's surface makes me want to paint it.

"Yeah, it's pretty alright." When I turn my head and catch him staring at me, I have to try really hard not to blush. Instead, I manage a shy smile.

Garrett clears his throat and readjusts himself on his saddle, giving me the impression that he's just as embarrassed as I am.

"And if you're thinking it's named after the color of the trees, you're wrong. There's an old copper mine that runs beneath it. Our family mined it for years."

"So all this is yours?" I feel overwhelmed by all the space around me. I knew the Carson family was rich before I came here. My mom wouldn't have contemplated marrying Bill if they weren't. But everything surrounding us suddenly seems to hold so much more value than money.

"Everything you can see belongs to the Carsons," Garrett confirms, "and I'll do whatever it takes to protect it." He makes that last part sound like a threat, and the determination in his expression confirms it.

"I don't doubt it," I smirk. He's still looking at me in that dark, yet alluring, way that makes my pulse quicken. And I rub my lips together when I wonder what it'd be like to kiss a man like Garrett Carson. I kissed a guy once before, but he was just a high school boy and the whole thing felt kinda forced, especially since we were at a party and had all our friends watching.

"So, where is this perimeter we need to check?" I change the subject when I feel the tension between us pull tighter.

"Just on the other side of the ridge," Garrett informs me, moving us on at a more steady pace. He sits so naturally on a saddle it's clear he was born to ride. If I thought watching him drive was sexy, watching him ride a horse is another level of hot.

I'd be lying if I said I didn't find the whole cowboy get-up attractive on him, which is good because I've quickly learned that it's very rare to see a Carson man without a Stetson on his head.

"So, has my brother taught you to canter yet?" he asks, with the tease of a smile on his mouth.

"No, not yet." I can't pretend I'm not pissed about that. I never was a patient learner, and Wade's whole 'learn to walk before you run' approach to learning sucks, especially considering the man rides wild horses for a living.

"You wanna?" Garrett has a daring smirk on his face that looks damn hot, and I could really get used to this playful side of him.

"It's been a while since Darcy here has stretched her legs. I'm sure she'd appreciate it," he adds, when I don't respond straight away.

"I'd like to try it, if you think it's safe," I check, and when Garrett suddenly pulls his horse and mine to a stop, he has a very serious look on his face.

"I'd never let you do anything that wasn't safe." The way his forehead creases together when he says that shows he means it, and I slowly nod my head, hoping I haven't ruined his mood.

"Okay then," the smile eventually returns to his lips. "You hold tight to that saddle." He warns, before making that click with his mouth and kicking on his horse, Darcy automatically sets off beside them, and we quickly build up pace.

"Grip the front of your saddle to hold your balance," he reminds me; and when the horses' hooves, thudding against the ground, start beating to the rhythm of my heart, I understand why him and Wade spend so much time on a saddle.

Despite it feeling strange to start with, I maintain my balance and relax. The whole experience is kinda exhilarating, and when I glance across to Garrett and see the smile on his face, too, it makes me feel really fucking good. Garrett doesn't smile all that

49

often, and to think that I might have played a tiny part in the reason he is now, fills me with satisfaction.

"So what are we actually checking for? " I ask, when Garrett pulls us to a stop in front of a long wire fence that seems to stretch for miles.

"All sorts of things. Gaps, trapped cattle, signs of a disturbance." He starts trotting the horses along the fence line, observing carefully.

"And what's the difference between here and the other side?" The land looks just as open and sparse as the one we're on now, and we're miles from any roads.

"This is ours, and that's theirs," He tells me with that serious look back on his face.

"And who are 'they'?" I question.

"The Masons," he looks annoyed at having to say the name. "They own a ranch on the other side of town, and that pretty boy who tried touching you up last night works for 'em."

"If they own a ranch on the other side of town, what do they want with the land here?" It makes no sense at all.

"Because here, land is power, and people like to own as much of it as they can. That land you see between us and that tree line is a hold that the Masons have over us."

"What kind of hold?" Now I'm really laughing. I fail to see what damage some open fields are gonna do.

"Suppose the Masons decided to build on it, or give permission for a road to come through. It could ruin us. I'll never understand what was going through my grandpa's mind when he sold it to them," Garrett shakes his head sadly.

"Maybe he thought you owned enough land," I look back over my shoulder, trying to remind him of what he has. The Carson ranch is huge, one of the biggest in the state, and they have at least five different herds. Well, that's what Mom was bragging about to all her friends before we came out here.

"Nah, he regretted it. I know he did," Garrett leans forward and rests his arm on the front of his saddle. "I was the one who found him swinging four days after he signed it over." His jaw tenses as he stares out at the land, and I see the pain on his face.

"I'm so sorry. That must have been terrible." I struggle to believe a man would take his own life over selling some land, but then, this world is one I'll never understand.

"There's more to it, and one day when I find out what it is, I'll put it right." He turns his focus on me again.

"I guess your land has to end somewhere. You can't own it all." I shrug my shoulders.

"You're right, but ours don't end here. We own another thirty acres beyond that tree line," he nods his head toward the woodland on the other side of the pasture. "And it's pretty much wasted since we can't drive a herd across there. You see why none of it makes sense, now?"

"Just ask the Masons if you can pass through," I suggest, and the immediate laugh Garrett makes holds no humor, just bitterness.

"Yeah, well, old man Mason ain't very neighborly. He ain't got a lot of sense, but he's got enough money to buy a town. He doesn't like people having more power than him."

"So sell the land on the other side. If it's no use to you, what's the point in having it?"

"Can't do that either," Garrett shakes his head. "That territory over there borders the reservation, and our great, great grandfather made a promise to their chief that he would never sell it or build on it,"

"In return for what?" I find myself genuinely fascinated by Garrett's little history lesson.

"In return for his daughter. The land was a gift from her father to bless their union. I guess none of us would be here if that union never happened,"

"You're serious?" This plot just got thicker, and I'm here for it.

"On my life, our great, great grandmother was from the reservation," Garrett explains with a hint of pride, and I guess it explains those handsome, chiseled features he's got.

"Years have gone by since then. The men must be dead. You can't seriously still be held to a word that was made all that time ago," I point out.

"But we do," he stares across the overgrown pasture, toward the tree line.

"Why?" I shake my head and try hard to understand.

"Because, if a man ain't got his word, Maisie," he pierces me with those dark eyes that make my pulse quicken, "what the fuck has he got?" Creasing his forehead, he angles the reins he's got in his hand to the left and turns his horse, and Darcy follows his lead when he clicks to get us moving again.

CHAPTER 9

GARRETT

"I've never been to a cattle auction before," Maisie almost sounds excited as we head towards Billing. I've seen a change in her these past few weeks. She's happier, and although we still get the occasional brat attack outta her, she seems to be adapting to the ranch lifestyle way better than I expected her to, which is more than I can say for her mother.

Cora's high maintenance, and since she's arrived she's thrown herself and my father right into the thick of Montana's upper society. I barely see him these days. He's always got a dinner to attend or some charity event that can't be missed. I guess it suits him, as he's always preferred the office to the outbuildings. For him, the ranch has never been a lifestyle. It's always been the reputation and power he wanted to uphold. He curses the name of my grandpa and Uncle Jimmer, for the way they used to run the ranch before he took over. But the brutal truth is, our family and the way we got shit done *was* the power. The land, the money, and the livestock that's just what the power protects.

"You're gonna love it, all those hot cowboys kicking up dust and showing off," Wade tells her. He's managed to make it home this week, which is proving to be handy since the ranch is busy and Pops is busy pandering to all Cora's demands.

"That's not how it is," I shake my head, saving the girl from disappointment.

"Oh yeah, that's right, that'll be the rodeo. Which, by the way, you still haven't come to watch." I realize I just loaded the gun for Wade to fire another shot at me. I've been promising to take Maisie to watch him in action for a while now, and I've not seen through on it yet. When Maisie gives me that disappointed look, I realize I'm going to have to give in.

"I'll make sure we're in Columbus next weekend," I agree, nearly swerving off the road when Maisie squeals and wraps her arms around my neck. She spontaneously kisses my cheek, and I have to take one hand off the wheel to keep my hat on my head.

When she realizes her reaction was a little too much, she backs down and shares an embarrassed little smile with me.

It's pretty. It's cute, and yet it feels fucking deadly. I purposely ignore the sly look my brother gives me from the other side of the truck.

I ain't in the mood for his shit today.

"So, what are we looking to buy?" Maisie's got a spring in her step as we cross the field where I've parked the truck and head toward the cattle pens.

"A decent bull," I explain, already starting to size up some of the stock that is in the stalls. If she's trying not to act disappointed, she's doing a real shit job of it. The frown she's wearing pretty much says it all.

. . .

"Hey, is that Dalton over there?" Maisie holds her hand over her eyes to block the sun and looks across the pens, "It is Dalton!" She waves her hand frantically at him to get his attention, and when he spots her he looks every bit as eager to see her as she is him.

Dalton's the same age as our sister, and he's worked the ranch since he was twelve years old. He's Mitch's nephew, and no one's ever had the balls to ask Mitch where he came from. Not even me. If my father hadn't stopped marking the bunkhouse boy's loyalty with our brand, Dalton would have had his years ago. Like Mitch, he ain't ever leaving the ranch.

He's got a childlike manner about him, but he works hard, and over the years, he's proven his loyalty to my family time and time again.

Wade's left him in charge of maintaining Maisie's riding lessons, which I have to admit pleases me a damn sight more than it would if he'd given the job to any of the others. I see the way they look at her, devouring her with their eyes and thinking their filthy thoughts. It makes me want to scrape their eyeballs out and bleach their brains.

"Boss," Dalton holds up his hat to greet me and Wade. Technically, I ain't his boss, but above Mitch, I'm the only one that gives out any orders. My father wouldn't have a clue who half the men working for him are these days. Which is just as well, considering.

"Miss Wildman," Dalton's eyes move fondly to Maisie.

"I've told you not to call me that," she laughs, and a pang of jealousy hits me right in the center of my chest.

"I didn't realize Tuesdays were your day off?" I query him. I'm not even sure Dalton has a day off.

"It ain't, sir, the Missus sent me,"

"The Missus?" I glance across to Wade, who seems to be sharing the same confusion I am.

"Mrs. Carson. I'm here to pick out a stallion for her to gift to Mr. Carson, for his birthday."

"She sent you?" Wade checks he's hearing right and does nothing to hide the shock from his face. There's no denying that Dalton knows a thing or two about horses, but when it comes to picking out good stock, I'd expect a woman like Cora to trust a more experienced eye to ensure she gets the right bang for her buck. What's even more confusing, is the fact Cora knew we were coming here today. We talked about it over breakfast, and I remember it vividly because I was trying to distract myself from the tiny tank top and non-existent pajama shorts Maisie decided to wear at the table. Sometimes I wonder if that girl knows the effect she has on me and does it on purpose.

Why didn't Cora ask us to pick something out for her? And why is she even getting Pops a new horse? The old man quit riding years ago.

"Garrett and Wade are here to look at bulls," Maisie tells him, with that unimpressed look on her face again.

"I'd much rather shop for horses. Can I go with Dalton?" When Maisie turns her attention to me and asks for permission, I get a sick little kick out of it. Even if that pang of jealousy comes back for an afterburn.

"Sure," I tip my head at her, doing my best not to seem bothered by it.

"You just make sure you have her back at my truck by 4," I warn Dalton, who agrees enthusiastically before holding out the crook of his arm for Maisie to take.

"I hope you find the bull you're looking for." She bites her lip and looks at me guiltily, as he leads her away.

I watch them move through the crowds together, heading over toward the stables, and when I catch Wade staring me down out of the corner of my eye, I quickly divert my attention and scan over the auction brochure in my hand.

"Seriously? You just lost out to fucking Dalton," he laughs at me, and I swear to God, I could wrestle him to the ground and feed his clever fucking mouth my fist.

"Lost out what? Wade, get your head out of your ass and help me look for a decent bull."

"So you're still in denial about it all?" He shakes his head at me.

"I ain't in denial," I move forward, still looking through the brochure and trying to locate the stall that holds the bull I've had my eye on.

Frustratingly, Wade's right and I'm far too distracted to focus. That niggle inside me has started up again, and despite it being unhealthy, I can't switch it off.

"You think she likes him?" I clear my throat, doing my best to make it sound like I don't care, but failing miserably. The fact I'm bothering to ask proves I fucking care.

"He likes her, but then, all the bunkhouse boys like her," Wade points out, fueling my agitation.

"What you heard 'em saying?" They all got a warning from me last week, when I overheard a few of 'em talkin' about her and didn't like what was said.

"Unholy things, brother, but I doubt it's anything you haven't thought of yourself," He tries to get a rise out of me, but I ain't biting. Instead, I get back to locating the bull.

"Ummm, Garrett," there's a sudden change in Wade's tone, and when his hand starts tapping at my shoulder, I look in the same direction that he is, and I see what's got him sounding so off guard.

"Is that Cole?" he asks, as we both stare across the stalls into the corner where the Masons always keep their stock. Sure enough, there's our brother leading in a heifer and wearing a red shirt with the Mason's logo sewn on the chest.

"*What the fuck?*" I cross my arms and watch him steer her into a pen.

The Masons have been our rivals since they came into town and bought out nearly every ranch within a fifty-mile radius, and the fact that our brother is working for them now doesn't just shock me, it pisses me the fuck off.

"I've got a good mind to go over there and…"

Wade sets off toward him, and I quickly grab a hold of his shirt to drag him back.

"Not here." I shake my head, somehow managing to keep my cool.

It takes a lot for Wade to lose his shit, and I fully understand that seeing our brother with them would be the cause of it. But there are some important people here, and today we're representing the Carson family and Copper Ridge. Cole is obviously representing *them*.

"We'll have it out with him, but not here," I speak tightly into Wade's ear, keeping my grip on him until I feel him simmer down.

I wait for Cole to look up, and when he spots us watching him, I put all my disappointment into the cold stare I hit him back with. I get that he's pissed at Pops, but this right here is the ultimate betrayal to our family, and I mean what I said to Wade, we will be having it out.

It takes a bidding war with Ronnie Mason, but I manage to get the bull I came here for, and while Wade navigates the handlers to load him onto our trailer, I lean against the hood of the truck, light up a cigarette and wait for Dalton to return Maisie.

He shows he's got some sense by turning up five minutes early, and when I see how happy Maisie is, I can't help but feel like he's stolen something from me.

"You should see the stallion Dalton picked out for Bill. He's not as big as Thunder, but he's strong, and he's…"

"Get in the truck," I cut her off, then hate that I'm the cause of the pretty smile slipping from her face. She does as she's told without any sass, and the fact that disappoints me too, has me questioning my fucking sanity.

"I'll see you back at the ranch, sir," Dalton lowers his head to me before he backs away, and when I get inside the truck, Maisie is sitting on the bench seat beside me.

"You didn't have to be so rude," she snaps, without pulling her eyes up from where they're fixed on her lap. She's making it clear I've upset her. But I don't react. I just wait for Wade to hop into the seat beside her, before I pull out and head for home.

CHAPTER 10: MAISIE

I thought we'd made progress when Garrett took me out for that ride a few weeks ago, but lately, it seems Garrett's been doing everything he can to avoid me. I don't like it, and the stubborn bitch in me wants to make it hard for him.

"Where are they?" I ask Dalton, when we're walking Darcy back to the stable after my lesson.

Now we're in the thick of summer, the bunkhouse boys are taking group shifts camping out to protect the herds from predators, and Garrett announced over dinner last night that he'd be joining them.

"We got a Long Camp out on grid four. They'll be staying around there," Dalton informs me.

"Could you take me there?" I ask, trying to make it sound more like a dare than a chore.

"I could, but I don't know if the boss would like it," he raises an eyebrow at me awkwardly.

"And who, exactly, is the boss?" I question.

"Well, technically, it's old man Carson, but Mitch is in charge of me, and Garrett is in charge of him, so…"

"Stay right there." I march off toward the main house, heading straight into Bill's office. He's at his desk where he usually is, and when I knock at his already open door, he looks shocked to see me.

"What a nice surprise," he stands up and gestures for me to sit in the seat opposite him.

"I'm not staying, sir. I just came to ask if I could ride out to where the boys are camping. I was gonna take them some homemade cookies,"

Bill doesn't need to know that there are no homemade cookies. I'm sure he's far too busy pen-pushing, to check up on me.

"I think that would be a very nice idea," he smiles, almost seeming proud. "But you mustn't ride alone, have Dalton or one of the boys from the yard ride out with you."

"Thank you," I smile, before I start making my way back out.

"And Maisie," Bill's voice commands me to turn back around.

"It's nice to see Darcy out of the stable again. It's even nicer to see her being ridden. Keep up the good work." The old man shows he's got a soft side after all, and I smile at him again before rushing off to find Dalton.

"Keep her saddled. We're heading out to grid four," I call out at him ,before he can put her away.

"Guess I better saddle up myself." He passes me Darcy's reins and rushes off toward the wrangler's stable to find himself a horse.

I had no idea how far away from the ranch grid four actually was, and I'm grateful when I see the tiny cabin in the distance. There are tents pitched up near it, and a campfire is lit, despite it being the middle of the day and sweltering hot. Dalton tells me it's to ward off those predators that they're out here protecting the cattle from.

"I can go from here by myself," I explain. I already have a

feeling Garrett isn't gonna be happy about me being here. And the last thing I want is for Dalton to get into trouble.

"I don't know, Miss, it's still quite some distance," he looks unsure.

"Look, it's open fields until the tree line, and I can make it there in a few minutes if I canter."

"And what if she throws you off?" he takes off his hat and scratches his head, still unconvinced.

"She won't throw me off. Will you, girl?" Reaching forward, I tap her neck confidently. "You can wait here and watch me if you want."

"Ok, I'll watch ya. Just make sure you take it steady."

I nod him a thank you and kick Darcy on. It feels kinda liberating riding through the open land all by myself, and when I reach the camp, I twist around on my saddle and wave Dalton off.

There are a few wranglers on horseback, making sure no cattle stray from the herd, but I can't see any sign of Garrett.

"Where's your boss?" I ask the big, mean looking one who's resting by the fire. I've seen him around the yard a few times before, and from the vibes he gives off, I figure he's not afraid of much, especially bears or wolves.

"He went spotting," he answers, before spitting at the ground. I don't like the way his eyes linger on my body. It creates a different kinda feeling to the one I get when Garrett stares at me. These eyes feel dirty on my skin.

"Which way did he go?" I ask, keen to move on.

He slowly tips his head toward the woodland and smirks, and when I kick Darcy on, and steer her into the trees, I feel him watch me leave.

I'm wary of the fact there could be wolves or bears as I ride through the trees, but there's something about being on horseback that feeds my confidence, and I make sure to keep my wits about me while scanning the forest for Garrett.

I head toward the sound of running water, and when I come to the river and see a horse tied to a tree, I laugh when I find one of the cowboys bathing.

Pulling Darcy to a stop, I sit back on my saddle and watch Finn toss water over his face. I never had him down as the type of guy to have tattoos, but his back is covered with a huge, hooded skull, and I tip my head to try and get a better look at it, so I can recall where I've seen it before.

"Like what ya see?" Finn catches me staring, and the smirk on his face suggests he doesn't mind too much.

"Aren't you supposed to be working?" I point out, trying to be clever.

"Taking a break, it's damn hot. You should join me," His eyes are daring, and never being one to back down from a challenge, I call his bluff, and slide off my saddle. Tethering Darcy up beside his horse, I brush my hands together and watch his face turn to shock as I head towards the water edge.

I look at his pile of clothes on the rock beside me and notice the rifle sitting beside it.

"What's the gun for?" I ask, kicking off my boots and unbuttoning my shirt. I have a tank top beneath, which I won't mind getting wet.

"What do you think I'd do if a wolf came out of those trees?" he smiles, and I suddenly realize what a stupid question that was. It also makes me realize how stupid I've been riding through these woods alone.

I pop open the button of my jeans and slide them off my hips. Then kick them to the side and move closer to the water. It's a little chilly when I dip my toe in, and Finn keeps that cheeky look on his face while I withstand the cold bite and force myself deeper.

The river flows steadily, and I wade through it as I head toward the middle where Finn is standing with the water up to his waist. I have to admit it does feel good, especially when I spread out my fingers and let the water run through them.

"You got a pretty smile, you should use it more often," he tells me, and I roll my eyes at his attempt of flattery. You can tell Finn's a typical cowboy. A love 'em and leave 'em type like Wade is. But he's close to my age and fun to be around, and there's something about him that reminds me a little of home.

"I smile plenty," I assure him, bending my knees and leaning back against the current to look up through the trees. The sunlight shines through them and heats up my skin, and when I hear Finn start to laugh, I quickly stand up straight again.

"You know, I think you like it here." He's wearing a smug look on his face, and despite it being handsome as sin, it doesn't match up to any of the expressions I've seen from Garrett.

"I got no choice in being here, so I might as well make the most of it," I shrug.

"That's the kinda attitude to have," he starts moving through the water to get closer to me, and my heartbeat picks up. He looks as though he might kiss me, and as handsome as he is, there's only one man here who I want to be kissed by. I gasp in shock when he slams his forearm hard at the water and splashes my face.

"You rat," I giggle, feeling a little relieved, then using both my palms I push some water back at him. He hits me with another faceful of water, and when I lose my balance on the stones beneath my feet, his strong arm quickly wraps around my waist to steady me.

Suddenly he breaks us apart, and when I turn my head to see what he's looking at, I see Garrett leaning forward with his elbow resting on the front of his saddle and a finger sliding over his lips. He's staring at me as if he expects an explanation.

"I'm sorry, sir. I was just taking a break." All the fun has suddenly vanished from Finn's voice.

"I can see what you're doing Finn, what I'm wondering is

what *she's* doing here with you?" Garrett's cold dark eyes remain fixed on me.

"I was... I just came looking for you." I sound so foolish, but I also notice that Garrett looks taken off guard by my answer.

"Finn, break time's over. Get back to the herd, and take Darcy with you," Garrett dismisses him. I watch him quickly wade through the water, and grab up his clothes and rifle before he jumps on his horse's back. He's still soaking wet, and when he reaches across to untether Darcy, I realize Garrett's instruction makes no sense.

"But how will I..."

"Maisie." The way he says my name with such authority actually stops me from finishing my sentence, and I remain standing in the water, with my head down, while I await his next order. It's unlike me to fall in line, I've always liked to push boundaries. Back in L.A. it used to get me in trouble, but Garrett has a presence about him that makes me want to please him.

"And how do you expect to get your clothes back on, now that you're soaking wet?" he asks eventually. I find the courage to raise my head and bravely look at him again, and he makes no attempt to hide the fact he's staring at my body.

"I guess I wasn't thinking about that at the time," I admit, pissed off at myself for being in this stupid situation.

"See, that there's the problem. Out here, if you don't think, you die,"

I close my eyes in shame, the tank top I'm wearing is sticking tight to my skin. and I can feel my nipples hard and poking through the fabric.

"I'm sorry," I force the words out, pissed off at the fact I feel the need to say them. I owe this man no apology, he has no right to control me, and yet he seems to hold authority over me that I can't explain.

"Get out," he shakes his head as if he's disappointed in me, then jumping off his horse he starts untying something from the back of his saddle.

I push through the water and step out onto the bank where he waits with a thick, tribal print blanket; and as he drapes it over my shoulders and pulls it tight around me, I can't help taking satisfaction in the contact. Once the blanket is fully wrapped around me, he holds it together tight in his fists and when I look up at the dark eyes that are staring at me from beneath the rim of his hat, he slowly releases me.

I stand here feeling helpless and stupid as he gathers my boots, jeans and shirt from the floor and ties them all onto the back of his saddle. He jumps back on it, then holds out his hand for me.

"Come on." There's no patience left in his tone, and he doesn't look me in the eye. It almost seems like he's ashamed of the gesture himself.

"You want me to get up there, with you?" I check.

"I'm taking you home so you can get dry," he explains, still waiting for me to take his hand.

Despite it being a hot day, my lips are trembling from the chill of the water, and I'm really not in the position to argue. Besides, I kinda like the idea of riding close to him.

I gradually step forward, holding the blanket around me in one hand and gripping the front of his saddle in the other. When I place my foot in his empty stirrup, Garrett reaches down and wraps his arm around me, then hauling me up, he makes room for me on the front of his saddle.

We're so close that I feel his warm breath against my neck, and as he takes the reins and makes a slow ride through the trees, I do all I can to distract myself from the way his hips rock against mine. The hand he's holding the reins in rests against the inside of my thigh, and it feels so intimate, I'm grateful my panties are already wet.

Garrett doesn't speak to me for the whole ride back to the

house, and I can sense his anger and feel the tension beating from his chest into my back.

"What about Darcy?" I ask, when we finally make it back to the yard.

"I'll have one of the boys bring her back," he answers me bluntly, before jumping off from behind me and gripping my waist, ready to lift me off.

"I could have just ridden her back my..." I go to argue, but he cuts me off.

"Do you realize how dangerous it is being out there by yourself?" He fires the words out his mouth like he's been holding them back for too long, as his fingers dig deeper into my waist.

His eyes are narrow and full of frustration, and it makes them even more appealing.

"I was only by myself for a little while. I saw Finn bathing in the river, and it looked like fun. Excuse me for trying to have a good time." I try to pull away, but he keeps his hands firmly in place, forcing me to listen.

"Well, that good time could have cost you your fucking life. I watched you both for a good five minutes before either of you realized I was there. Supposing I was a predator. Do you think Finn would have got to his rifle fast enough...? Out here, there's no such thing as a good fucking time Maisie!"

The way he snaps at me makes my stomach twist. I won't have him get away with talking to me like that, and all the anger on his face quickly turns to shock when I shove him hard in his chest and force him off me.

"Maybe not for you, but there are some people in this world who intend to enjoy life," I rip off his blanket and thrust it at him, and the way his shocked eyes stare down at my body reminds me of the very little I'm wearing. Yes, my top may have become a little see-through from the water, and yes, I am standing in the middle of the yard in my panties, but I will prove to Garrett Carson, and myself, that he can't control me like he does everyone else around here.

"I'd thank you for rescuing me *if* I actually needed rescuing, but the only thing you saved me from today was fun." I turn away from him, then somehow manage to untie my boots and clothes from the back of his saddle before I storm past a startled looking Dalton back to the house.

CHAPTER 11

GARRETT

I wait until she's inside before I march into the stable after Dalton. He looks fearful when he sees me coming, and I grab him by the front of his shirt and shove him against the stall door.

"Who saddled her up and let her leave?" I've been holding back my temper the whole ride home, and now it's about to get unleashed.

"That would be me, sir," he looks down at the ground ashamed of himself, and so he fucking should be. Anything could have happened out there. She wasn't armed, and even if she was, she wouldn't have had the first clue on how to fire the damn thing.

That's something I'm gonna have to rectify.

"It was cleared with your father, sir, and I rode her all the way to the Long Camp. Never let her outta my sight,"

Dalton can be trusted, he has no reason to lie to me, but this doesn't explain how she ended up half naked in the river with Finn.

"From now on, when it comes to the girl, the only person you take orders from is me. You understand that?"

He nods back at me slowly, and I give him one final shove before I head back out and re-mount my horse.

I can sense her watching me from her bedroom window, but I don't look back, instead I set off on the ride back to grid four, so I can figure out who's ass I'm gonna have to kick for sending her into the woods alone.

Usually I enjoy spending a night under the stars, there's nothing quite like hearing a fire crack and listening to the bullshit stories wranglers make up to impress each other. Yet tonight, all I can think about is her. The way her top and those panties stuck to her body is a sight I won't be getting out of my head for a real long time, and I'm pissed about the fact I have to share that image with Finn.

When I found out who was to blame for sending Maisie into the woods alone, I decided to make an example of him. I dragged Seth off his horse and kicked his ass, and now he's tied to a tree down by the river with open wounds, hoping that any bears and wolves roaming ain't hungry tonight.

I wait for Finn to come back from being on patrol with Tate. He'll have heard about what happened when I returned to camp, and I'll bet he's waiting for his own punishment to be served. I stand up off the cabin porch and dust off the back of my jeans, gesturing my head for him to step inside. I figure he knows what's coming because he sure looks worried.

I follow him in, and he starts to grovel before I've even closed the door.

"Look, I know you've spoken to the others about how she ended up in the woods alone, and I want you to know that it had nothing to do with me. She was already riding through when she saw me. She just stopped to talk…"

"And ended up in her underwear," I finish his little story for him, folding my arms across my chest and waiting on an explanation,

"Well," he shrugs his shoulders, and the smirk on his face is far too cocky for my liking.

"That was the girl's choice. It's been a hot day, and she was looking to have some fun," he's grinning at me like I'm his fucking friend now, and when he notices the cold stare I'm coming back at him with, he quickly loses his confidence.

"I... I didn't realize she was off limits, sir, and anything that happened between us, you saw for yourself," I shut him up with a fist to the jaw, and it doesn't surprise me when he takes it like a man. Finn's good stock, he ain't afraid to get his hands dirty, and although he's only been here a short time, he's naturally become one of the wranglers we rely on. It's one of the reasons he ain't tied to the tree next to Seth.

"She. Is. Off. Fucking. Limits," I make my point abundantly clear for him. "You, or any of the others, so much as *look* at her with an intention, and I swear to whatever you believe in, I'll send you to it's hell."

"Gotcha, boss," he nods, wiping the blood from under his nose.

"Now, we're gonna talk about that tattoo you got on your back." I was too busy being mad down at the river to react, but I saw his Dirty Soul tattoo. My uncle formed that club over thirty years ago when he abandoned his father and brother and left this ranch, and I can't help being curious as to how one of their members has ended up here.

"My father was a branded man, he left to join the Souls with your grandfather's blessing. I was raised among them, but that's all in the past now. I'm where I belong," he assures me.

"Yeah, well, pasts like that tend to come back at ya. And if my father saw that tattoo, you'd be off this ranch faster than a bull out the chute,"

My uncle hasn't given a shit about this ranch since he walked away from it. It's highly unlikely he'd be giving a shit now. Finn came here on Mitch's recommendation, and I know he stays in contact with Uncle Jimmer. There's no coincidence in this situation, but I trust Mitch with my life. I just don't appreciate him keeping this from me.

"I won't ask you about it unless you give me reason to suspect your intentions."

"I ain't got no intentions, sir," Finn assures me. Up to now he's given me no reason to doubt him, so I'll offer him my trust. He'll be the one to suffer if he makes me regret it.

Most would class our world as a million miles away from the lifestyle of the bikers… but those who live it, and have to defend it, know differently. The purest of man can become an outlaw if he finds something worth fighting for.

I dismiss Finn to join the others and take a seat in the corner of the room, helping myself to the stash of whiskey that's tucked away in the cupboard beside it.

Mitch tells me my grandfather built this cabin and that Pops was lying when he told us it was built for night watches, like this one.

No one ever fucked with the Carsons because the consequences were too great, and I'll bet a lot of those consequences happened here. It all started going wrong when Jimmer left town, my grandfather held on as long as he could, and I always wondered if losing that respect was the reason he took his own life. Then came my old man, who decided he wanted to do things differently. He wanted to be legit, and I've spent too many years watching him fail.

If this ranch stands any chance of still being here in ten years time, changes have to be made now, and I figured out quite a while ago that I was gonna have to be the one to make them.

I sit alone and stare at the floor, and for the first time in a long time I focus on something other than trying to fix it. I think about how it might have been if I were the one throwing Maisie around in the river earlier today, instead of Finn.

I wonder how it would feel to make her laugh like she ain't got a care in the world, the way Dalton always seems to. And I torture myself imagining what it might have been like to touch her under those wet clothes.

I failed today when I gave into my own temptation, but seeing her like that made me desperate for contact. I made Finn take her horse, just so I could have her close to me. So her body would touch against mine, and I don't know if she noticed it, but I smelt her hair all the way back to the yard. It takes me a while to figure it all out, and when I do I feel the crush of devastation. It turns out all this anger I got constantly brewing inside me when I'm with her, or even just thinking about her, ain't anger at all.

It's envy.

The girl's got her whole life ahead of her, and as much as I'd like to sit here and fantasize over how it could be. I owe it to her to make damn sure it never becomes a reality.

It's the only way I can keep her safe.

CHAPTER 12

MAISIE

It's three days before I see Garrett again, and that's only because I purposely stay up late waiting for him to come home. It's almost midnight when he eventually walks through the door, and he looks exhausted, covered in dirt and dust.

"You missed supper," I get up from the couch, where I'm resting, and walk towards him.

"Josie will have plated me something up." He takes off his hat and hangs it up, before heading into the kitchen. I follow him through and watch him check inside the microwave. There must be something in there because he sets the timer and rests his hands on the counter, dropping his head between them and breathing out a heavy breath while he waits for his food to heat up.

"Tough day?" I do my best to make conversation, even though I can sense he isn't looking for company.

"It's always tough." He stretches his neck from side to side and rotates his head.

"You must like it, you're the only one stupid enough to stick around."

He doesn't respond, not with words anyway, just a cold stare that suggests I'm being a nuisance.

"I wanted to say sorry, about what happened at the river the other day," I decide now is as good a time as any to apologize. "I spoke to Mitch yesterday, and he told me some stories. If I'd heard them before, I'd have never ridden through the woods by myself. I get why you were mad at me,"

Garrett says nothing, just nods his head.

The loud ping of the microwave interrupts the awkward silence, and taking out the plate, he sets himself up at the breakfast bar, ready to eat.

I move over to the refrigerator and take out two beers, twisting the cap on one and placing one in front of him before I open my own.

"What's that for?" He stares at the bottle.

"It's a peace offering," I explain, leaning over the breakfast bar and noticing his eyes drop into the v of my sweater.

"Ain't no need for it," he flicks his eyes away when he realizes I've noticed, then keeping his expression blank, he takes a drink.

"I was mad at you at the time, but after thinking about it, I figure it's nice to have someone looking out for me. I don't know if you've noticed, but my mom isn't exactly the caring type."

He must find that amusing because he sniggers, and since it makes me feel more at ease around him, I pull up a stool and continue.

"And I've never known my father, he took off when I was a baby,"

The way he frowns suggests that he feels sorry for me, and that's not the way I wanted this conversation to go.

"Our folks left town again. They've gone for a spa weekend over at that new development," I explain, in case he's wondering where they are. He looks a little shocked, but in the spirit of friendliness I decide not to press him on it.

"This is such a big house. It's easy to feel lonely here," I point out, thinking about how insane I've been driven by being on my own all day.

"Maisie, what are you doing?" Garrett drops his fork, and when he looks up at me impatiently, I suddenly have no idea what to say.

"I don't know," I shrug. "I guess it felt a little sad to think you'd been out there working all day and didn't have any company at the end of it." I hadn't realized until right this second that that is exactly the reason I'm here, that and the fact I think I've missed him.

Garrett has no come-back. He just stares at me with that same shocked look on his face.

"Yeah, well some of us ain't got enough time to feel lonely," he pops a forkful of pork chop into his mouth, and while he's chewing on it I get the last word.

"Or maybe, you're just not used to company," I suggest.

His eyes focus on my lips, and I wonder if he's ever thought about kissing them. I think about kissing him all the time, and I've already decided that Garrett Carson kisses like a movie star.

He must have some kind of superpower that makes up for the fact that he's making it damn impossible for me to be nice to him, but I persevere and remain seated opposite him until his plate is clean. He stands up to put it in the sink, and my eyes automatically follow him across the room.

"You should get to bed. We got an early start tomorrow." He looks out of the kitchen window across the yard as he speaks. "Truck's leaving at eight and not a minute later," he warns in that harsh tone that I've come to really like.

"You mean we're still going to the rodeo?" I can't contain the excitement in my voice, and when Garrett looks over his shoulder at me, I feel a whole different kind of excitement fizzle in the pit of my stomach.

"I made ya a promise, didn't I?" He very almost smiles, and instead of running at him and throwing my arms around him like I want to, I manage to compose myself.

"I'll see you in the morning," I head for the door.

"Maisie," I turn around far too quickly when he calls me back.

"Thanks for waiting up." He speaks the words so quietly I only just hear them, and I nod my head at him before leaving the room.

CHAPTER 13
GARRETT

It's hard not to stare at her, especially when she's looking the way she is.

The denim cut-offs she's wearing are far too short, and the red checked shirt she has knotted at her midriff shows off just enough of her tight stomach to make me want to kiss her there.

She can't hide how excited she is and when she's excited, she smiles a helluva lot. I try not to like it, but it's not easy. Making her happy does something to my insides, and I can't help but like that she doesn't seem angry about having to be here anymore.

"You ever do anything like this?" she asks, as we make our way onto the stands. The arena's packed out today, just how Wade likes it. He's sure to put on a good show.

"Yeah, I wasn't bad at it," I shrug my shoulders. Sure, I never made it to pro like Wade has, but I was a strong competitor.

"Why don't you do it anymore?" Maisie's big, blue eyes look even prettier when there's a spark of curiosity inside them.

"Things got too busy on the ranch, Pops injured his back and struggled managing all the day-to-day running, so I had to step up." Her bottom lip pouts out, and her forehead creases like she's feeling sorry for me, but there ain't no need. I like working the ranch, there's no place I'd rather be, and I'm not afraid of hard work.

"You take on a lot, you know," Maisie looks out onto the ring to avoid eye contact with me.

"Yeah, well, someone's gotta," I huff a laugh, and roll up the programme I got in my hands.

"Just 'cause you're the eldest doesn't mean you have to do everything."

"I don't do *everything,* we have staff."

Granted, some of those staff have been questionable choices. Seth survived his night in the woods, and after Mitch untied him, he got sent on his way. Now I'm a man down, and in the middle of summer, that's a helluva strain.

"You have another brother. Can't he pull his weight?" she suggests.

"Cole's complicated, he can't be pushed. He's angry right now, best thing to do is leave him to do his thing." What I want to tell her is that Cole's a selfish bastard, he knows how much stress I'm under. Pops sits behind his desk, thinking he's mastered success, while I'm doing everything it takes to claw some of our respect back.

It's stubbornness, and hate, for his brother that keeps Pops from seeing any sense. The way his pa ran the ranch was what kept it successful. Uncle Jimmer had the same vision, he knew that to stay on top you gotta be a little underhanded. You gotta have control, and the Carsons used to have anyone who was important in their pockets. Men wore the Copper Ridge brand because they were proud to belong there, now all those men have gone, and Mitch is the only branded man left on the ranch. He's a man of his word, and despite disagreeing with my pops, his loyalty to my grandpa, and that brand on his chest, keeps him here.

The years without control have taken their toll, and Copper Ridge has become vulnerable. Whether or not it's fair, it falls on me to make sure we push back.

Maisie gets distracted when the evening starts, and despite all my attempts not to, I spend most of the time watching her.

"Who's he?" she asks, when the seventh rider climbs into the bucking chute, and the crowd starts to cheer.

"That's Leonard Mason, three time world champion," I tell her, there ain't no denying he's good, but he got to where he is on bribes and backhanders. The Masons were new to ranching when they arrived in Fork River, fifteen years ago. Pops said they would never last, but they've bought everything that surrounds us, and it seems the town eats out their hands, instead of ours, these days. Even the Mayor and the Commissioner, who claim to be friends with Pops, fall in line with their demands. I was too young back then to prevent it from happening, and I'll never forgive my father for sitting back and watching them take from us.

"He's really good." Maisie watches him gripping the saddle and fighting to stay on the bronco. I hate that she looks so enthralled by him, it puts a kinda anger in me that I ain't used to. One I know can't be relieved, not even if I kicked the ass out of Leonard Mason, myself.

"88.5," the announcer calls out, and she jumps to her feet and cheers like the rest of the crowd.

"Looks like Wade's up next!" She looks down at me excitedly, when she spots him climbing over the bucking chute. It always makes me nervous watching him, my brother is damn good, but he's reckless. You gotta be a certain kind of man to get on the back of a bronco. One without cares and without feeling. Back when I used to ride, I used to love that countdown. Time stands still when you're fighting to stay on a saddle, your hands go numb, and the adrenaline pumps through your veins so fast you hear the blood rushing in your ears. Despite all the chaos around you, there becomes an emptiness inside your head. In those few seconds, all that matters in the whole world is staying on the back of that horse.

My heart beats hard in my chest when the gate opens, and I tense as I watch my brother get thrashed around by the strong-willed bronco he's saddled on. He makes it look effortless, and I swear I see the hint of a smirk as he passes the 6-second mark.

"He's incredible." Maisie watches him in awe, and it's pathetic how jealous it makes me feel.

"Wow... We got a 90.5, ladies and gentleman. Wade Carson makes it to the top of the leaderboard with 90.5!" The crowd goes wild, and when I stand on my feet to join them, I stumble back when Maisie throws her arms around my neck and kisses my cheek. It's just like she did in the truck, on the way to the auction, last week. Only this time instead of holding on to my hat, I let it fall, and I wrap my arm tight around her waist just so I can test out how it feels.

Her eyes fix on mine when I keep her held, for a little longer than I should. We're so close, close enough, that I could test how it would feel to kiss her, too, but it doesn't matter how much I want to. It would be wrong. Maisie Wildman is off limits, not just to the bunkhouse boys but to me, too.

I release her slowly and sit back down, picking up my hat and dusting off the rim before I place it back on my head. She looks disappointed, but still manages to give me an awkward side glance and a sad smile.

I'll just have to ignore how much it fucking hurts.

In the end, Wade takes the buckle, and when we head around to the trailers to congratulate him, Maisie can barely contain her excitement. She runs at him and embraces him the same way she did me, and when he lifts her up off her feet and kisses her cheek, I have to look away.

"You were awesome! You just beat a world champ!" she

squeals, and as always, he does a shit job of acting modest about it.

"I've beat him before, and I'll beat him again," he tells her, before looking over at me.

"Good job," I nod my head. Wade knows I'm fucking proud of him.

"We're all heading over to Henley's Grill to kick back, you wanna come?" he asks, and I can tell by the look on Maisie's face that she wants to go.

"I gotta get back to the ranch," I feel bad for pulling her away, but I have no idea what time Pops is planning on getting back from this retreat he took Cora on, and I promised Tate he could have the night off, which means I'll have to take his watch.

"I can give her a ride back. I was planning on coming home tonight anyway," Wade offers.

"No, it's fine, I came with Garrett." The sheepish, little smile she gives me makes my chest feel fucking heavy.

"You should go have a good time," I tell her; as much as I want to spend the drive home smelling the way the breeze pulls through her hair, like it did on the way here, she shouldn't have to suffer for it.

"You mean it?" There it is again, that natural instinct she has to seek my approval. And it's so fucking wrong of me to get off on it.

"Go have fun," I tip my head at her, then look at Wade. "A word," I gesture my eyes toward the trailer, and he follows me behind it.

"You watch her and make sure she stays out of trouble."

The pathetic smile, he looks back at me with, makes me want to punch him. "I mean it Wade, she ain't from round here. Keep your eye on her,"

"I got ya, brother," he slaps my shoulder. "You heard

anything from Cole?" The cocky smirk drops off his face, and he suddenly looks serious.

"Not a thing," I shake my head. Fuck Cole. He ain't worth getting a headache over, not when I've got so much else to figure out.

"His funeral, he'll come crawling back, and when he does, we'll make him eat shit," Wade laughs, and I roll my eyes before heading back to say goodbye to Maisie.

"Can you really not come?" She wrinkles up her nose and pulls that disappointed face at me.

"I really can't, but you have a good time," I go to walk away, and when she calls out my name desperately, I immediately turn back around.

Her eyelashes flutter, and she blushes like she's embarrassed by her outburst.

"Thank you for bringing me," she bites her bottom lip and smiles at the same time. And I have to get the fuck outta here before I march back over to her and take it between my own teeth.

I think about her all the way back to the ranch, trying to remind myself that I lost a sister eighteen months ago. I never really grieved Breanna, but to do that, I'd have to get past all the anger I got for myself. I can tell myself as many times as I want that I'm looking at Maisie like a replacement, but it won't make it true.

The truth is I'm a hypocrite, I'm falling for a girl fourteen years younger than me, and I'm counting down the days until she goes back to her life in L.A. so I don't have to suffer it anymore.

When I get home to the ranch, the yard looks empty, and I head straight for the stable to saddle up Thunder, so I can go relieve Tate. The guy works hard, he deserves a break, and a distraction from the thoughts in my head is needed right now. I can't think about what she might be doing, or who might be watching her. I just gotta hope that Wade sticks to his word and takes care of her tonight.

"Garrett," I turn around when I hear Tate's voice. He's dressed up, looking like he's heading out for a good time

"I think you're gonna wanna see this," he hands me his phone, and I can tell by the look on his face that I'm not gonna like what I see.

I stare at the photo that's been sent, and the blood boils under my skin.

"Noah sent it. Apparently he's back in town, staying at the B&B," he informs me.

"He's got some fucking nerve." I pay closer attention to the photo of Laurie Cross. I gave him some work here, two summers ago. Our whole family was a mess back then. I was a mess, but I couldn't show it. Someone had to hold everything together. I had to put a lot of faith in the men who worked for us, and I made the mistake of putting some in him.

Laurie left the ranch, with a trailer full of steers and he never came back. And now, it seems, he's got the balls to show his face in town.

"I'm figuring I'll be taking my night off tomorrow?" Tate sniggers at me.

I hate to let him down, but I can't let this lie. Cross took advantage of my trust. To let him get away with it, is just an invitation for someone else to do the same.

"You want me to come with?" he asks.

"No, we're short on numbers at the camp. I got this handled." I assure him, tapping Thunder on his shoulder before lifting off the saddle I'd just thrown on him.

"I'll get changed and head back there now," he smiles at me like it ain't a problem and I nod my gratitude, before I head back to my truck.

I sit in the darkness of Laurie Cross' room, waiting for him to come home. The Taylor's guest house is cozy and welcoming; and it still survives, despite the bigger hotels that have been constructed in our neighboring towns. Some people want the small-town experience, and when it comes to development, this town sticks together.

Grahame Taylor owes me a favor, so he was happy to see me inside, and in return, I told him he could reassure his wife that I wouldn't leave a mess behind.

It's late when Laurie stumbles inside the door, and the woman that comes in behind him gasps in fear when she notices me sitting in the chair by the window. I'm pretty sure it's the same girl Wade fucked at the street party, the town threw, on the Fourth of July.

"You better get going, sweetheart," I warn her, leaning forward to rest my elbows on my knees and enjoying the way Laurie starts to panic.

The woman doesn't even bother to say goodbye, just clutches her purse against her chest and rushes out the door.

"Garrett, I…"

"I figure you came back into town to pay me back for what you stole," I interrupt, before he starts with the bullshit.

"I… I came because my mom's sick and she can't afford the medical bills. I'm looking for work, and I'm told the Mason's are hiring. If I can get work, I can look at paying you back."

I nod my head, like I might believe him for a while.

"See, that's confusing because, I'm sure you told me that your momma died when you were a teenager," I remind him.

His face turns white, and the way he fidgets with his hands tells me I'm right. "So were you lying to me then, or are you lying to me now?" I ask calmly.

"I'm… I just need the money, Garrett." Laurie lets out a long, desperate sigh.

"And you really thought you could show your face in this

town, after stealing from us, and not have to pay any consequences?" I scratch at my stubble and snigger.

"I'm desperate. I got three kids living in this town. I got maintenance to pay, and I wanna their father. Kelly's already moved in with her new guy, and it's only a matter of time before she tries to phase me out.

Those kids are all I got, Garrett. Please." I rest back in the chair and light up a smoke. I can see the man is desperate, but that don't mean he can get away with what he's done.

"I'll do anything, anything. Everyone knows what you're about Garrett. I don't mind doing some dirty work to pay off my debts,"

"Dirty work?" I laugh. "I couldn't trust you with a trailer of cattle; you think I'd trust you with the *dirty work*?" I crush out my smoke, stand up and walk towards him, watching the fear in his eyes grow wider.

"I'll take the brand," he blurts out, and it makes me pause.

"There ain't no brand anymore." I have to take my eyes off his when I say that because I know how disappointed my grandfather would be to hear it. "Besides, to be branded, you gotta be trusted, and I'd rather put my bare dick in that whore, who just walked outta here, than put any trust in you."

"So what ya gonna do? Kill me?" Even in the darkness I can see his fear, and when I reach up to take his throat in my hand, I squeeze so hard that I make him choke.

"I gotta be honest, Laurie. I'm seriously fucking considering it," I tell him, and mean every word.

I've always had a hunger for pain. I can't remember when it started, and I can't see it ever stopping. With me, there are no limits. I've killed men for doing less to my family than Laurie Cross did, but I've never made orphans outta innocent kids before, and I certainly ain't about to start. Laurie starts to struggle, it's a feeble attempt to save his life, and I use the hand I'm not crushing his windpipe with to punch him in his face and knock his pussy-ass fight, right outta him. He cries like a baby, blood and dribble spills from his mouth, and when my eyes catch the picture of his kids that's on his bedside table, I let him go.

He falls to the ground with a loud thump, clutching at his throat and spluttering like a dying dog.

"You wanna keep your life, you're gonna have to do something for me," I light myself a fresh cigarette and look down at the pathetic mess at my feet.

"Anything, I told you. I'll do anything."

"I want you to make sure you get that job on Mason's ranch, and I want you to feedback anything you think would be useful for me to hear."

Laurie manages to climb onto all fours, and I lay my boot into his stomach to knock him back down.

"I wanna know what my brother's doing there, and I wanna know how he's getting treated." I crouch down and blow the smoke, from my lungs, into his face and watch as he nods his head at me.

"This is your chance to show me that you regret what you did. Fuck it up, and I'll kill you." I promise, then stretching back onto my feet, I slam my boot into his face before I walk out the door.

I get back to the truck and notice three missed calls on my phone. They're all from Wade, and I immediately start to panic as I call him back. Starting the truck, I wait for him to pick up.

"I lost her," he answers, sounding worried. There's a lotta noise coming from the background, and I'm struggling to hear him.

"What do you mean, you fucking lost her?" I yell down the phone, slamming my palm into the wheel of my truck before I scrub it over my face.

"I mean, I went to the john, and when I came back out, she was gone. Garrett, I don't know where she is. She was hanging with Jason, they looked like they were getting on, and he's not here either,"

"Have you tried calling her?" I pull out of my parking space and start heading back toward Columbus.

"Course I have, she ain't picking up, and neither is he."

I don't know who the fuck Jason is, but the thought of him touching her is making me murderous.

"I'm on my way," I tell him, hanging up the phone and pushing my foot harder on the gas pedal. I don't give a shit about the red light I run through. All that matters right now, is finding her.

It only takes an hour to get there, and when I storm into the dive bar where Wade told me they'd be, I breathe a sigh of relief when I see her sitting beside him. What I don't like is the fact there's another guy resting his hand on her shoulder. A guy I'm guessing is *fucking Jason.*

"You called him?" Maisie looks at Wade and rolls her eyes, like she's mad at him for it.

"I panicked," he holds up his hands in defense, before swiping his bottle off the table and drinking from it.

"You ok?" I ignore the guy standing beside her and focus my eyes on her. She doesn't appear to be injured or harmed in any way.

"She was feeling a little light-headed, so I took her out for some air," he informs me, and when I look from her to him and see him grinning back at me, it makes me want to fish-hook each side of his mouth and tear it apart.

"Ain't you a fucking hero?" I grin back sarcastically, before looking back to Maisie.

"Come on. I'm taking you home." The harshness in my tone is still there when I hold my hand out for her, but instead of taking it she scowls at me.

"I'm not ready to leave," I don't know if she's a little drunk or just back to being the sassy girl she was when she first arrived, but I'm not in the mood for games.

"Maisie, I drove an hour out here to pick ya up. We're leaving." I try and keep the rage out of my voice, but when the girl shakes her head at me, I feel my patience reach its limit.

"I don't think she wants to go, buddy," Jason pipes up, and my brother instantly goes from being chilled to on edge.

"What did you just call me?" I stare at his friend, as all that rage travels straight to my fists.

"Hey, Jase, why don't you head over to the bar and get more beers?" Wade pulls a wad of notes from his jeans pocket and presses them into the guy's chest. He's trying to avoid a situation, so I'm figuring he doesn't want Jason, here, to get hurt.

"You want something, darlin'?" Jason proves he's got some balls when he strokes his hand through Maisie's pretty, blonde curls and watches for my reaction while he does it.

"Oh shit," Wade utters under his breath, and I don't give Maisie a chance to answer the asshole's question before swinging at him.

I put him straight on his ass, and the fact he don't get back up makes the pain in my knuckles worth it. My brother just looks at the floor and strokes his forehead.

"Get in the truck." Maisie looks stunned when I point at the door, and not in an impressed way. She doesn't move. She doesn't speak, just flicks her eyes between me and the cock-sure cunt that I just laid out on the floor.

"I said get in the truck. We're leaving." A circle of people have gathered around us, and I can feel all their eyes drilling into the back of my head. Maisie stands up, stepping closer to me and the way she licks those lips of hers makes me clench my fists.

"I'm not going anywhere." Her voice comes out seductive, with the hint of a dare.

"That's where you're wrong. I *said* we're leaving." When I raise my finger and point it at her, I wonder if anyone else notices that it's shaking. The girl's playing a risky game, my anger holds no bars, and tonight ain't a good time to be testing it.

"Whatcha gonna do, force me outta here?" She tilts her head like a temptress and finalizes my decision.

"If that's the way you want it." I move toward her, hauling her up by her thighs, and tossing her over my shoulder like a bag of wheat grain. Naturally, she protests, slamming her fists into my back and wriggling her body to try and get free of me. I tense the arm I got wrapped around her thighs, tighter, and withhold the urge I got to slap her ass as I carry her out of the bar and toward my truck.

I don't know if Wade's following, I don't fucking care, and when I place her feet back on the ground, I use my hips to force her against the side of my truck and keep her pinned while I open the passenger door. Her hands try to push me away, and when that doesn't work, she beats her palms against my chest and calls out all kinds of curse words. I rip open the door, and when I grab her face in my hand and force her to focus on me, she suddenly gives up the fight and goes silent.

"Pretty girls shouldn't fucking curse," I growl at her. Her chest rises and falls against mine, and my eyes are unable to focus on anything but those lips I'm desperate to kiss.

It would be so fucking easy, and the look in her eyes tells me that she wants me to. But instead of giving in to temptation, I release her, standing down and giving her enough space to get inside the truck. She doesn't try to run, she doesn't argue, she just grins at me like she's the winner of the game, I didn't know I was a competitor in, then hops her ass into the passenger seat.

Turns out Wade didn't follow after me, so it's just me and her on the journey home. And we're only a few miles out of Columbus when she breaks the awkward silence.

"So, you think I'm pretty, huh?" she makes her voice sound

so mocking, that I have to grip the wheel. I decide not to give her taunts a reaction, she's had enough outta me for one night.

Instead, I keep my eyes on the road and turn on the radio so I can blank her out. But it proves to be fucking impossible. She has her phone out and is smiling as she scrolls. I can't help wondering what it is that's making her look so engrossed. Is it him? Did she message him to see if he's ok? Maybe it's Wade or one of the friends back home, that she's so desperate to get back to. Either way, it ain't fucking me, and my level of envy at that only confirms that my obsession with her is getting outta control.

It's after midnight when I pull into the ranch, and when I stop the truck outside the house and cut the engine, neither of us make any attempt to get out. We sit in a dark silence.

"Thanks for coming to get me," she eventually speaks up. It sounds a lot like she's changed her attitude, and when she shifts across the bench seat to be closer, I feel myself start to panic. I don't know how much she's had to drink tonight, but her confidence seems to have grown. I don't look at her, just focus my eyes on the speedometer in front of me and count slowly in my head.

"And if it matters to ya, I think you're kinda hot, too." She leans in even closer, her lips almost touching my ear. "Especially when you get mad," she whispers, before pressing them against my jaw. It takes all the restraint I have to stop my head from turning and making those lips fucking mine, and I wonder if she feels the tension shaking in me as my knuckles turn white from gripping that fucking wheel, like my life depends on it. If she does, she doesn't mention it. She just slides away from me, opens her door and gets out. I watch her strut in front of the hood, moving toward the front door, then glance over her shoulder at me and smile before she lets herself inside. Then I look up and curse God for putting something on this earth so perfect and not allowing me to have it.

CHAPTER 14
MAISIE

Over the weeks, I've come to learn Garrett's morning routine. He wakes up just before six and takes a shower. Usually he's in there for around twenty minutes, and I often wonder if this is where he relieves himself. I mean, all men do it, right?

I'll bet Garrett looks hot as hell with his cock in his hand. It's bound to be big, too. Everything about Garrett is big.

I lie with my head on the pillow, staring at the ceiling and thinking about last night. Him calling me pretty felt like a victory. It also confirmed all those suspicions I've had that he's holding himself back from me, and now that I know I'm not the only one with an attraction, I can start to have some fun.

What Garrett did last night was completely out of order, and the fact I liked it isn't what's important here. What is important is that he laid down the foundation for the game. Now it's time for me to show that I want to be a player.

When I hear the running water shut off, I get out of bed, and check my hair before I head out to the hall. The door to the bathroom is closed, and before I attempt to twist the handle, I take a deep breath for courage. Garrett is temperamental, I never seem to be able to gauge what mood he's in, and I really hope that today he's in the mood for this.

Thankfully the door is unlocked, and the room is full of steam when I step inside. Garrett is at the basin, wearing a towel wrapped around his waist and the water droplets on his back make his skin glisten. He's brushing his teeth, and frowns at me in confusion through the reflection of the mirror when he realizes I've let myself in.

I watch him spit into the basin, keeping his eyes on me suspiciously as I head toward the shower. He doesn't ask me what I'm doing. He doesn't tell me to get out. He just stares.

His dark hair is wet and hangs over his forehead, almost covering his eyes. His shoulders are broad and strong, and thanks to the mirror, I can appreciate the dark line of hair that starts at his belly button and trails beneath the towel. He shows me no weakness, and gives no reaction, so I decide to up the ante. I'm about to cross the line, and despite being nervous about it, I somehow manage to hold it all together. I grip the hem of the tank top I'm wearing and slowly lift it up my body and over my head. Garrett doesn't remove his eyes from our reflection, despite the fact I'm now standing completely topless in front of him. He continues to scrub his teeth, and even when I smile at him, he keeps his eyes stern and expression hard. Next I slide my hands into the PJ shorts I'm wearing, shimmying them off my hips so that they drop to the floor; and the mouthful of foam Garrett spits into the sink comes out a little more aggressively, but his eyes still don't move.

I watch him swill his mouth out, then grip the basin in his hands and lower his head.

Is it cruel that I enjoy his suffering?

Am I crazy for poking the bear?

I watch his shoulders heave up and down, and the reaction I'm getting from him puts a tingle inside me that feels a little too desperate to maintain. Turning my back on him, I step around the glass barrier and turn on the faucet. Whether he loves me or hates me for it, I'm pretty sure I just guaranteed myself a place in Garrett Carson's thoughts for the rest of the day.

The water comes out at just the right temperature, and I let it soak my hair and warm my skin. I'm feeling powerful until I turn around, and the breath I take turns into a gasp. Garrett stands in front of me with a scowl on his face. His fingers grip around my throat and he forces me against the glass panel behind me.

"You should be careful, little girl. Keep fucking teasing, and I might just bite." His threat sends a shiver over my skin, and as the water pelts over his head, dripping through his hair and onto my body, he looks between us and studies every inch of me. I want him more than I want to take my next breath. And the strain I feel in his fingertips tells me he wants me, too.

I can feel his cock's hard, under his drenched towel, because it's pressing against my stomach. Yet, I'm not afraid of it. I want it. I want it to be him who takes my innocence. Right now, it feels like it already belongs to him, anyway.

"I mean it, Maisie, stop the games," his forehead presses into mine and breathes me in, like he's allowing himself a little fix. I close my eyes and wait for him to give in to the pull between us. And when I feel his touch slip away, it makes me want to cry.

CHAPTER 15
GARRETT

Soon as I'm dressed, I march outside toward the woodshed. I skip breakfast. Wade never came home last night, and Pops and Cora aren't back from their trip yet, which means it would be just me and her. I can't face that, not after what she just put me through in the bathroom.

What the fuck was she thinking, coming in like that and taking off her clothes? It only confirms that I ain't doin' a good enough job at hiding my feelings. She's using my affection as a fucking weakness, and it's working.

Dalton is already here chopping up wood and stacking it to dry out, ready for winter, and I make him jump out of his skin when I come up from behind him and snatch the ax right out of his hand.

"Go find something else to do," I growl, slamming the ax hard into the log in front of me. I don't know what to do with the build up of aggravation inside me. That ball of tension I've been carrying around in my chest, since she got here, just keeps on swelling, I can feel the binds that hold it in pulling tighter, and it's only a matter of time before they snap. I grip the handle of the ax tighter in my hands and slam it into the wood over and over again, praying for some relief. And when it doesn't come, I throw the ax into the wood, head around the back of the building outta sight, and I have to physically bite my fist to stop myself from screaming.

I had a good mind to take her, right there, in that fucking shower. It's what she wanted. She was practically begging me for it. I'm sure I would have been her first. I could have been all she's ever known, and the thought of that, makes me crave her all the more.

"You ok, son?" I spin around and when I see Mitch, I quickly straighten my hat and pull back my control.

"Yeah, I'm good. Just caught my thumb under a log, that's all," I shake out my hand, acting like that's the thing that's fucking hurting, and the old man seems to buy my bullshit.

"Heard Laurie's back in town." He rests his shoulders against the shed and lights himself a smoke.

"Yep,"

"He's one cocky son of a bitch, I'll give him that." Mitch shakes his head and chuckles to himself, as he holds out his packet for me. "So, how d'ya handle it?" I can already tell he ain't happy that I handled it alone. Mitch likes to get involved with these kinda things.

"I kicked his ass, and then I put him to work." I light up my smoke and rest the back of my head against the wood cladding, breathing out and trying to get the vision of that naked body out of my head.

"You offered him a job?" Now Mitch is looking confused.

"Not here. He came back to town because his kids are here, and he was looking for work over at the Mason's. So that's where he should be, right now. We'll figure out soon enough if he's learnt anything about loyalty."

"And what if he ain't?" Mitch don't sound too optimistic.

"Then I'll kill him," I smile, before throwing my smoke at

the ground and crushing it under my boot. Time to get back to work.

It's midday when Wade's truck pulls up in the yard, and I excuse myself from talking to the farrier so I can catch him before he goes inside.

"Mornin'," he lifts his hat and smirks at me.

"Thought you were coming home last night?" I point out, noting that he's still wearing last night's clothes. I assume he left the bar with one of the girls who were clinging to his ass like horse flies.

"I had a better offer," he winks, "I'm sure you understand why I'd rather have ridden a couple of barrel girls, than take the long ride home with you two?

What the fuck was that, back there? Jason's a good guy, he weren't doing no harm."

I can't explain it to my brother, not without him taking triumph in it.

"I had a hard night. When I got back from the rodeo, Tate was waiting for me. He told me Laurie was back in town. I'd just finished dealing with the asshole when you called."

"Is he...?" Wade checks around the yard for anyone who shouldn't be listening.

"Not yet, I had a use for him."

"What use could you possibly have for a disloyal bastard, like Laurie Cross?" he laughs.

"The only use you can have. I'm relying on that *disloyalty*."

Wade must be too hungover to try and figure it out because he shakes his head.

"And what ya gonna do about her?" he points his head over my shoulder, and when I turn around and see Maisie sitting on the porch, I have to quickly look away. Just lately, she's started dressing to fit in around here, and the pretty, little summer dress she's teamed up with a pair of cowgirl boots has me wanting to haul her over my shoulder again.

"I ain't gonna do shit. Just ride out the summer."

"Bet you wish you were riding it out on her?" He tries not to smirk but can't help himself, and I can't even react because I know she's watching, and she's seen more than enough violence outta me since she's been here.

"That's not the answer to everything, Wade, and it sure as hell won't make the pain go away." I hurt him with my words ,instead. Me and him both know that fucking has been Wade's therapy since Breanna died. He don't ever talk about her, but I know he blames himself just as much as I do. It's a burden me and my brothers will carry until the day we die.

"It makes it go away for a little while," he shrugs.

"You should try it sometime, ain't nothing like a meaningless fuck to clear your head," he steps in a little closer to me, "but something tells me that with her, you're scared it wouldn't be meaningless," he whispers.

"That ain't the reason," shaking my head I try to convince myself of that, too.

"Oh yeah, then tell me what is?" Wade pulls away and rests against the hood of his truck, folding his arms like a cocky prick.

"And remember, we're past the denial phase now. You knocking Jason out last night and dragging her out of that bar gotcha over that hurdle."

"Fine," I check back over my shoulder, and it's a mistake because seeing her sitting on the porch step, clenching a mug of coffee, just reminds me of all the reasons why I fucking want her.

"Number one, I'm too old for her. She's *fucking eighteen*, Wade, and you see the look of disgust on people's faces when they see Pops and Cora together. You think I want that for her?

Do you think I want her to have to face people, judging her the way they do her mother?"

"That's a piss poor reason. What else you got?" he frowns.

"Ok, the fact our parents are married to each other. I'm pretty sure that's not fucking ok, either." Wade shrugs, but I can tell it's not enough. "And…" I take another glance at her and feel that squeeze in my chest again. "Look at her, she's beautiful, and despite the way she sometimes acts, she's innocent. That girl is naïve to all the shit that goes on around here, she has no idea of the kinda man I can be. I like that, just the way it is."

"You ever wonder if you've focused so much on this place, that you've never taken the time to figure out what makes you happy?" he questions. "I'll ask you again. What's it all for, Garrett? What is this place, if there ain't a family to keep it for? Who do you work all those hours for? Who do you think of, when you beat the crap into the bastards who try screwing us?" He narrows his eyes because he thinks he's getting somewhere.

"I'm thinking about *our* family," I tell him.

"Garrett, you know as well as I do, that our family broke the day you found Grandpa swinging from those rafters," his eyes glance over to the outhouse where I found him, and I can't even follow them and look over there myself. I haven't been in there since, and don't care if that makes me a coward.

"He quit on us. Mom quit on us when she fucking left, and Breann…"

"Don't you fucking say it!" I hiss through my teeth, and shove my finger at his face. I swear the boy will never saddle a fuckin' horse again in his life, if he does.

"Bree didn't fucking quit on us. She was crying out for fucking help, and none of us heard her. She was just a girl, we all should have been there for her."

Wade's eyes drop to the ground, proving he's ashamed of himself.

"Don't mean you don't deserve to be happy," he finally looks up.

"Maybe you're right about that, Wade, but I sure as hell won't be forsaking someone else's happiness for my own. Even *I'm* not that fucking selfish." I leave him to it, and head toward the stable, so I can saddle up Thunder and ride the hell out of here.

CHAPTER 16

MAISIE

"That looked intense," I smile at Wade when he steps onto the porch. He sits down on the step beside me and taking off his hat, he rests his elbows back, and blows out a breath.

"Tired?" I smirk. We were having a pretty good time last night until Garrett showed up and killed the party. Wade has something about him that draws people in. He's fun-loving and carefree, but I can sense that underneath all his smiles he can be vulnerable, too.

"He likes you, you know?" We both watch Garrett come out of the stable, leading Thunder, and the look he gives us across the yard as he mounts him, suggests that he's fully aware we're talking about him.

"I like him, too." It feels surprisingly good to admit that out loud. I'm still angsty from what happened in the shower this morning. The heat between us, and the need he's left inside me, is beyond frustrating and the fact he wasn't at the breakfast table earlier pisses me off, too.

"Pops called earlier, said him and ya mom are on their way back. They want us to have a family dinner tonight."

"That'll be interesting." I look at Wade, and we both laugh.

"Just give him time. He needs to figure his head out. It's tough when you like someone, and you can't have 'em."

"You sound like you're talking from experience." I take a sip of my coffee and can't help being intrigued. Wade could have any girl he wants. He's handsome, charming and rides the rodeo, for god's sake.

"Yeah, I got experience in it." He sighs and focuses on the hand that's playing with the rim of his hat.

"Wanna talk about it?" I offer.

"Not today. Today I wanna ride this pounding outta my head. Fancy saddling up? I'll take ya somewhere real pretty." I like that he's smiling again, and seeing as Garrett's made it clear he wants to avoid me, I decide I should take him up on his offer.

I have to canter pretty fast to keep up with Wade, and it takes about an hour before he stops at the edge of the river and dismounts his horse. I've never explored the north side of the ranch before, and I'm speechless when I take in my surroundings. The open grass around us goes on for miles, and the mountains in the distance are the perfect backdrop. We're on the other side of the ridge that Garrett took me to a few weeks ago, and when I close my eyes, the only thing I hear is the sound of the water rushing down the river.

"This, right here, is everything he fights for. I thought, if you saw it, you might understand. Hell, sometimes we all need a reminder."

"It's beautiful," I open my eyes and take it all in again. There's nothing but fields, mountains and trees. No boundaries. It reminds me of being a kid again, when there were no obstacles and no limits. I've always liked to draw or paint. I can go anywhere I want when I have a brush or a pencil in my hand.

And looking out at all the open space around me, makes me feel like I could ride Darcy all the way to the end of the earth.

"It is, but it can also be a curse to a man like Garrett," Wade leads his horse to the water's edge so it can drink, and I slide off my saddle to lead Darcy there, too.

"When you have something this beautiful, you can guarantee there will always be people who want to take it from you. You gotta stay on your guard and learn who you can trust. It don't matter how many fights you win; you're always gonna be at war," Wade says thoughtfully, tethering both our horses and taking a seat on one of the fallen trees. I take a seat beside him, sensing that he wants that talk, after all.

"A Carson man can get so wrapped up in protecting this place they lose sight of what's important. I think Garrett's scared that that's what'll happen to him. It's why he doesn't act on his feelings for ya."

"He barely knows me. He hasn't even taken the time…"

"He knows you well enough," Wade interrupts me with a clever smirk, "I'll bet he knew the second he locked eyes on you. Something shifts when it happens. It's weird. You feel your heart get shut off from the rest of the world. At first, you try to deny it. Then you try to ignore it, but it never goes away. And eventually, it becomes a curse. Just like everything you see here. A cruel curse disguised by beauty." Now I know Wade is talking from experience, and I want to know who it is that's cursed him.

"Garrett's lucky. When summer's over, you're going back to L.A. and there's gonna be helluva distance between you. He'll throw himself into working this place. Maybe he'll find a woman to settle down with and try to love her. But there'll always be nights when the whiskey won't drown out the pain, and creating hurt for someone else stops easing your own. Those'll be the nights he lets himself think about you." Wade pulls his eyes off the water, to look at me. "He'll wonder what might've happened if he got over his own stubborn ass and asked you to stay. And it will become the torture he lives for."

Wade sniffs and wipes his hand under his nose, "Anyway, enough about that shit. I brought ya out here to look at a pretty view, I didn't mean for it to turn into a deep and meaningful one."

"Who is she, Wade?" I beg him to tell me.

"She's a breath away, but a million miles out of my damn reach," he tosses a stone into the water and laughs, pretending it doesn't hurt him.

"I don't believe that. I think you could have any woman you wanted. You're a good person. I don't know what I'd have done around here, if it weren't for you," I nudge his shoulder with mine and make him laugh some more.

"See this, what me and you have? It's all I am to her. I'm her friend. I'm the one she calls when she needs someone she can rely on. I ain't ever gonna be more than that, and if it's all I can be, I'll take it. Some days I think it's a blessing. She deserves more. It takes a special type of woman to love a Carson man," he stands up.

"Do you think I got what it takes?" I take the hand he holds out, to help me back onto my feet.

"Oh you got what it takes, alright," he rolls his eyes and laughs, before grabbing the horses and helping me back on my saddle.

We don't talk much on the ride back to the house. I figure Wade has said all he needed to say, and I'm pleased he felt like he could confide in me. We trot back into the yard, and I notice the shocked look on Wade's face when he sees the truck that's parked next to his. I recognise the man standing on the porch. I saw him the day me and Mom arrived here. It's Cole, the Carson brother I've never been introduced to.

Wade slides off his saddle, keeping his focus on his brother, and when I do the same he hands me his reins.

"Take these into the stable and get Dalton to settle 'em," he instructs, suddenly seeming distant, and when I see Garrett approaching Cole from the other side of the yard, I can sense the atmosphere between them all.

As intrigued as I am by it, I decide I'm much better off doing as I'm told, so taking Darcy and Wade's horse, Hooter, into the stable, I leave the brothers to it.

Dalton greets me at the stable door looking equally as concerned by what's happening, as he takes the reins from my hands. I don't want to interrupt the little reunion that's about to take place, so I decide to help him.

"She stretch out her legs today?" Dalton taps Darcy's back, as he guides her to her stall.

"Sure did. I'm getting quite good," I tell him confidently.

"She likes it," he informs me.

"Tell ya that, did she?" I giggle, watching him undo the belt strap from under her belly.

"Course not, horses can't talk. But you can read 'em, and Darcy here, she's taken on a new lease of life since you arrived."

"Shame not everyone has, huh?" I think about all that Wade just told me, and although it kind of explains why Garrett constantly pushes me away, it doesn't resolve the situation.

"I think you remind her of Bree," Dalton smiles to himself as he hangs up my saddle, and when he notices the shocked look on my face, he starts to panic.

"Sorry, Miss," he cowers, like he's said something unforgiving.

"Don't apologize. Did you know her well?" I soften my tone, so he feels at ease.

"As well as any guy, who lives in the bunkhouse, is allowed to know the boss's daughter." Grabbing a handful of hay, he shoves it into the net that hangs over the stall door. "She was feisty, and stubborn, but she had a good heart. Always found time for me." He shrugs his shoulders, before moving over to Hooter and starting the same process.

"What happened to her?" I ask, becoming more desperate for answers.

"Ain't my place to say; just know that it was devastating for everyone. I've never seen my uncle cry before, I spent a lot of years thinking he was dead inside, and when he broke the news to everyone in the bunkhouse, there weren't a dry eye there, either."

"It must have been hard."

"Still is. Always will be." The way his eyes glass with tears make me wonder if Breanna was his curse. "If you're looking to avoid the shit show that's about to go down out there, you're welcome to hang with me in here. I gotta break due, and some coffee on the stove. I promise these folk don't create no drama." When he looks around the stalls at the horses, we both laugh.

"Sounds good to me," I agree.

CHAPTER 17

GARRETT

I've just gotten back from checking on the camp, and when I see Cole's truck parked up in the yard, I immediately see red. Jumping off Thunder's back, I stomp towards where he's resting his shoulder against one of the beams keeping up the porch.

"You got a fucking nerve showing your face here," I call over, spotting Wade coming in on him, too, from the corner of my eye.

"Don't speak to me about nerve. Not when you got Laurie-fuckin-Cross spyin' on me." Cole shakes his head, and I contemplate knocking it off his goddamn shoulders.

"I sent Laurie Cross to keep an eye out on this family's enemies. Ain't my fault you choose to work for them." I point out, my voice shaking with rage. "Now, get your ass back in your truck and fuck off back to the Mason's bunkhouse."

"That ain't much of a welcome home, now is it?" he chuckles, and Wade grabs him by his shirt and forces him up against the house.

"You gone deaf, as well as fuckin' stupid?" he spits at him, and I can see that the fury in his eyes ain't come from anger; it's from hurt and betrayal.

"This place is goin' under. Face it, it's over. You can't compete with the Masons; not the way Pops wants to run things. It's only a matter of time before he gets desperate and sells out to the corporate giants."

"That ain't gonna happen. Not while I got breath in my body," Hell knows how I'm staying so calm, maybe it's for Wade's sake, or maybe it's because deep down, I know what Cole says is true. We're treading water, and it doesn't matter how much money's in the bank, if these people want something they'll find a way of getting it. And it's looking like it'll be my generation that lets our family legacy down.

"Leave it, Wade." I place my hand on his shoulder and ease him down.

"You could have left town, you could have taken your trust fund and set up your own ranch in fuckin' Texas for all I gave a shit, but why there?" I ask, doing nothing to hide the hurt from my face. He caused it. He earned it, so he can face up to it while he gives me his answer.

"You wouldn't understand." He looks away from me, proving he's ashamed, and so he should be. He knows Uncle Jimmer leaving the ranch, all those years ago, had a massive impact. Soon as we were all old enough, we made a pact that we would never let that happen to us. We even made a lame-ass attempt to brand ourselves, like some of the bunkhouse boys.

Wade, being the youngest and having to go first, still got the scar on his arm to prove it.

"I'm your fucking brother, Cole. I'll make myself understand."

"I came here to tell you that you don't need Laurie Cross. If there was anything that I thought would put this ranch in danger, you'd be hearing it from my mouth. And if you sent him to keep an eye on me, you should know better. My loyalty will always be with you. I just got my reasons for being there, right now."

"I hope they're treating you like shit." Wade shakes his head at our brother, curling his lip in disgust as he barges past him and heads inside.

Cole pulls himself back together and takes a seat on the porch step. I sit beside him and notice his shoulders sag, like he's carrying the weight of the world on 'em.

"Tell me it ain't her, Cole." I beg, because shit's complicated enough between us and the Masons.

"I could tell ya it ain't, but I promised you I'd never lie to ya, so I won't."

"Fuck!" I slam my fist into the beam, beside me. "She's a married fucking woman, Cole!"

"Yeah, but she ain't a happy one." He stares at his hands, so he doesn't have to look at me.

"She made her choice," I remind him.

"Yeah, because I didn't give her no other one. And now she's suffering for it. I can't stand by and watch her get hurt."

"That's *exactly* what your fucking doing, by being there. And what use are you to her there, anyway? There, you're just a wrangler, nothing but a cowboy. Come home. You can make the difference, here."

"We're all just fucking cowboys, Garrett," he laughs bitterly. "You got the fight of a lion in ya, but the damage has already been done. We're gonna lose this place."

"We ain't. I promise. Pops is gonna see sense soon enough, and I got plans for when he does. Hell, I've already started working on things, you know that. Just come home, be part of it." I hate that I sound so desperate, but I don't want to do this without him. We've already lost so much, I don't want our loyalty to each other to be the next loss.

"I can't, Garrett, and I know that hurts ya, because it hurts me, but I can't watch this place fall around us. She's gotta know I'm there for her."

"Wade's right, they must be treating you like shit over there." I know for a fact those Mason brothers will be getting off on the fact he's working for them. I know I'm right from the way he clenches his fists.

"She's too scared to leave him, and for as long as she's there, I'll be there, too. I came here to make sure you know that that don't mean I've deserted my loyalty to you."

"You realize what'll happen if they figure out what you're doing? They'll already have their suspicions about you."

"I know the risks," he assures me, and when I think about Maisie and how much it hurts not to have her, it helps me understand him a little better.

"Pops is having a family dinner tonight; you should come, make the effort."

"I can't, I got work to do, and I won't sit around the table playing happy fuckin' families, watching the old man with her." He stands up and wipes his hands on the back of his jeans.

"You know she's never coming back, right? If Breanna dying didn't bring her home, there ain't nothing that will. For all we know, she could be dead."

"Maybe it'd be easier if she was," he admits sadly, and when my head nods in agreement, I hate myself for even thinking it.

"I need to know we're ok. You and that knucklehead are all I got, and I'm not asking you to support what I'm doing, just to try and understand it," Cole says.

I watch Maisie backing out the stable, wearing Dalton's hat on her head. She's swinging a bucket in her hand, and after she's filled it with the hose, she sprays him with it. Dalton reaches out, offering to help her carry the bucket back inside, and I watch her tease him with his Stetson when he tries to get it off her head. The sound of her laughter travels across the yard, warming my heart, and breaking it, all at the same time.

"I understand it," I assure my brother. "Just remember to take care of yourself."

"And what about him?" Cole's head tips toward the door that Wade just stormed through.

"He'll come around. He's just scared of losing another person he loves."

Cole nods his head and starts heading back toward his truck.

"Hey, whatever it takes," I call after him, because I want him to know I got his back. Yeah, what he's doing is stupid, but I can relate to it. I feel nothing but fucking stupid these days, and Maisie's only been here a little while. Cole's been crazy about Aubrey since we were kids. Our moms were best friends, and we always used to play together growing up. They dated all the way through high school, and although nothing shocked Fork River more than my grandpa hanging himself, Aubrey marrying Joe Mason came a close second.

The fact my brother stood by and let it happen shocked everyone, even more. Especially me.

I think back to the time when I told her that the tooth fairy wasn't real and made her cry. Cole lost his shit and split my lip, and it earned us both extra chores for a month.

Cole opens the door to his truck and raises his hat at me.

"Whatever it takes," he nods back, getting inside and pulling away.

CHAPTER 18

MAISIE

"Where are you going now?" I ask Mom, when I catch her wheeling a suitcase toward the front door.

"The Carmichaels invited us to spend the weekend with them at their lake house." She answers my question just as Bill steps out of his office, buttoning up his jacket.

"There you are. You look lovely, sweetheart," he kisses Mom's cheek, and she blushes like a teenager.

"You were away all of last weekend, and I only have a few more weeks before I have to go back to L.A. I thought it would be nice for us to spend some time…"

"Yes darling, and we will, but the Carmichaels hold a really influential seat, and if Bill wants to be a candidate next year, he needs those kinds of connections. Oh, and speaking of connections…" she hands me a piece of paper from her purse.

"That's Leia Walker's number. The Mayor's daughter. She's a lovely girl, a little older than you, but she's got your number, and she's going to invite you over tomorrow night. I'm told not many in town get the honor of an invite to her parties, so you must be very excited." Her attempt to rally some enthusiasm from me falls flat.

"Aren't I a little old for you to be setting me up on play dates?" I hand back the piece of paper.

"Maisie, you are going to that party. You can't afford to decline an invitation like that," she snaps back at me.

"*I* can't, or *you* can't?" I question. "I'm not gonna be here much longer. I have no intention of making new friends here. I have friends in L.A.," I remind her, granted it's been a while since I bothered to contact them. I've been far too busy trying to get Garrett's attention, but I see no point in making the effort when I'll be leaving so soon.

"And let's not forget who will be paying your college fees and living costs so you can go back home," Mother speaks through a tight smile, reminding me that we came here with absolutely nothing. "Mayor Walker is the kind of man Bill needs on his side. Fork River may seem like a small town, but he's a big fish." She fakes a motherly gaze at me when she takes my hand in hers, and presses the paper back into my palm.

"We'll be back Sunday night, darling," Finding her calm, she leans in to kiss my cheek, and Bill nods me an awkward goodbye, before they set off out the door.

I head back upstairs toward my room, already feeling bored. Wade left for a competition last night, and Garrett spends all his time out on the ranch with the wranglers these days. Now that Mom and Bill have left, I'm home alone, and when I pass Garrett's bedroom door and find it ajar, curiosity has me pushing it open a little wider. It's intrusive and a touch stalker-like, but I figure I may not get another opportunity like it, so I decide to take a look inside.

The interior is very similar to mine, and Garrett doesn't seem to have a lot of personal belongings. A few trophies in his windowsill and a couple of rodeo buckles.

I open his wardrobe and slide my fingers over his clothes; it smells like his aftershave in here, and taking the cuff of one of his shirts, I bring it up to my mouth and kiss it. Next time he wears this one, I'll know, and it will give me a little satisfaction.

I sit on his bed to test his mattress, it's much firmer than mine, and I imagine he likes it that way, there's nothing soft about him. I lay back and rest my head on his pillow, and when I look up at his ceiling, I wonder what he thinks about when he lies here at night.

Does he ever think of me?

Since I've been here, all I think about when I'm in bed, is him. I've even forgotten about missing my friends and how much I didn't want to be here. If he does think of me, I wonder if he ever touches himself like I do.

The need is there, just thinking about it. My pussy starts throbbing and leaks a little into my panties when I imagine him stroking his thick, long cock through his hand. I close my eyes so I can picture it. It's even easier now that I know how big he is. I felt it touch against me through his towel in the shower, the other day, and with that vision in mind, I give into temptation, and lift up my dress. My hand slides into my panties, and my fingers touch the part of me that aches.

I imagine it's his fingertips touching me as I take in the scent of him from his pillow. Stroking over my sensitive flesh, and edging myself toward that satisfying feeling of contentment. I imagine the weight of him on top of me, his breath in my ear and his skin touching mine and, when the sound of his throat clearing sounds a little too real to be in my imagination, I force my eyes open. I want to die when I see him, his shoulder resting against his door frame and eyes fixed on me. I can only judge, from his relaxed posture and the fact he has his arms crossed, that he's been there a while.

"Shit. I'm... I," I sit bolt upright, and feel my cheeks burning.

"Keep going," his forehead creases even more, and when he

pushes himself away from the doorframe and starts stepping closer, I can't decide if he's angry at me or getting off on my embarrassment.

More heat rushes to my cheeks. My heart beats like a drum, and I have to remind myself to breathe.

"I'm sorry, I was just…"

"I said, keep going," he repeats slowly, his voice remains low and calm, and he watches intently as I give in to his order and lay back down, placing my hand back inside my panties.

The way he tilts head and bites his lip as he scrutinizes what I'm doing, makes me want to give him more. So I push my panties down my legs and kick them off the bed, so he has a full view of me.

Maybe I should feel exposed or humiliated, but I don't. I feel alive, and having all his attention on me like this has me burning inside.

"What were you thinking about?" He edges a little closer to the bottom of the mattress.

"I was wondering what it might be like to have you touch me," I tell him honestly, as my fingers continue to rub against my clit, creating the friction I crave from him.

"And did it feel good?" Gradually he leans his body over mine, propping himself up with one hand and taking his hat off with the other. He carefully places it on the mattress beside my head and looks down his nose at me.

"Yes, it felt good," my lips tremble, and my fingers apply a little more pressure.

"Don't go too fast," he shakes his head and talks so soothingly, that I start to regulate my heartbeat again. "I want you to make it last a while," he whispers.

"Okay," I smile and nod as I take in his instruction, slowing my fingers into lazy circles.

"You ever had a man inside you, Maisie?" His lips are so close to mine I could easily reach up and kiss them, and I have to shake my head to answer his question because I can't form words.

All I can do is will him with my mind to take over what I'm doing, with his own hand.

"You ever put a finger inside yourself?" he asks next, and I hear the tension in his voice

"No," I swallow thickly, when I realize where this is going.

"I bet you're throbbing on the inside, right now. You should try it." When I nod my head back at him, he creases his forehead deeper.

"Then do it. Take your finger, and slowly push it inside your pussy," he leans into my ear, and his breath against my skin feels like sunshine on a winter's day.

I take his instruction, slowly pushing my index finger into my pussy and stroking myself on the inside.

"It's tight, isn't it?" Garrett slides his nose along my jaw, and when his lips touch my ear, I shiver. "Does it hurt?"

"No, it's a little uncomfortable, but it doesn't hurt." I use my thumb to massage my clit, to keep it from pulsing.

"Can you take another one, stretch yourself a little more?" There's a strain in his voice that tells me he's making himself suffer.

"I can do that," I assure him, inserting another finger and moaning as I feel myself stretch around it. It's a little sore, but Garrett is the perfect distraction, and when I glance up and see him looking down on me with those dark, heavy eyes, I wonder why he makes me suffer, too.

"You ever come before?" he asks, looking between our bodies and watching me work myself. I shake my head, feeling ashamed to admit it. I'm eighteen years old. None of my friends are virgins anymore, and barring touching myself a little, like I was before he caught me, I have no experience with these kinda things.

"You could give your first one to me. I think you'd like that," he growls, and I nod my head far too enthusiastically.

He pulls back, and when he wets his lips, I wonder if this will be the moment that it happens. I swear that all the tension that's built up inside me will erupt into something incredible, if those lips touch mine.

I close my eyes and wait, but that moment doesn't come, and the ache inside me grows heavier and harder to bear.

Garrett's forehead touches mine, the same way it did in the shower. "Let me have it," his voice commands, and just like he flicked a switch, my body jerks. My head spins as I throb around my fingers, soaking them with pleasure, and I grab hold of his bicep through his shirt with my free hand, when I feel like I'm falling. It lasts longer than I expect it to, and his body remains tense and taut above me as I moan and lose all my control.

When it's over, I open my eyes and breathe, having no idea how the atmosphere will be between us now we've shared something so intimate.

Garrett still has that serious look on his face, and when he sits back on his knees, I watch in shock as he takes the wrist of the hand I just pleasured myself with, and raises it to his lips.

His eyes remain fixed on mine when he takes my two fingers inside his mouth and sucks them clean. Then leaning back over my body he picks up his hat and places it back on his head.

"No one ever forgets the first time they come, Maisie," he promises me, forcing himself off the bed and walking out of the room.

CHAPTER 19

GARRETT

I should have left her be, I could have shouted at her, or sent her out of my room in disgrace.

I should have done anything other than what I actually did.

I've been so restrained. I've held myself back to the point of choking on my suffering. Now I'm here with the taste of Maisie Wildman's first ever orgasm on my lips, and more frustration than I can stand, rooted in my soul.

I head straight for Grandpa's garage, it's the last place anyone will ever expect to find me. And right now, I need to be alone.

I don't know when the last time someone came in here was, but I can tell from the dust and cobwebs covering the sheets on his vintage bikes, that it's been a while.

I look up at the rafter where I found him swinging, when I was nineteen years old, and my stomach rolls. That's how long it's been since I came in here, and I'm not afraid to admit it's because what I saw scared me.

I've seen some horrific things, I've done 'em too, but seeing that a man like my grandpa had given up on living was, by far, the worst of 'em.

He was the strongest man I ever knew, built like a mountain and smart as they make 'em. There wasn't a single person in Fork River who didn't respect him. Men wanted to wear his brand. They wanted to prove to him that they were worthy of the honor, and they wanted to be a part of the dynasty our family built over the years. Finding him that day, made me realize that there ain't no one in this world that's indestructible.

I thought nothing would ever scare me more than that. Even losing Bree didn't frighten me; it hurt like hell and made me fucking angry at myself, but not scared.

Yet the girl lying on my bed right now, with all that desire and hope in her eyes, petrifies me.

I want to scream, and I want to run, but I got nowhere to run to. So instead, I throw my fist at the beam in front of me. I hit it again and again, until my knuckles split open and my blood stains the wood. The pain comes, but it ain't enough. The frustration's still there, and I have to admit to myself that, for as long as she's here, it ain't going away.

I've never wanted anything the way I do her. My head can't understand it, and my body can't endure it. What I just let happen was bad for both of us. It's becoming harder and harder to control myself around her, and I know all this only leads to one outcome.

Fucking heartbreak.

There's no such thing as a perfect life. It's impossible to have it all; my grandfather and my pops proved that. For this family to keep this ranch and regain its respect, it has to be run by someone who has no other commitments. This ranch has to be the love of your life, someone has to make the sacrifice, and I decided thirteen years ago when I found my grandpa in here, that I'd be the one to make it. I just didn't realize then, that sacrifice would have to be her.

"Been a long time since anyone's come in here," I spin around when the door creaks open and wipe my bloody hand under my nose when I realize it's Mitch.

"I'm good, just needed some time alone." I stare down at the mess of my fists and try to breathe myself calm.

"It's the girl, ain't it?" he croaks, taking a seat on one of the dried-out hay bales and lifting off his hat,

"Yeah, it's her." I figure it's pointless lying to him, the man practically raised me, and he knows me better than my own brothers.

"She likes you, too, and she sure is pretty. I reckon you could convince her to stay." He dangles his hands between his knees and talks as if that's the fucking problem, here.

"That's the last thing I wanna do." I let out a bitter laugh, as I pace the ground in front of him and try to get my head straight. "She needs to leave and go to college, and the further she can get from here the better."

"Do you mean the further she gets from here, or from you?" he questions, and when I stop pacing and stare him down, I can't deny that a part of that's true.

"You've been here long enough, Mitch. You've watched every Carson man in the last decade, who's tried to run this ranch, fail. We can't have it all."

"Now, who says that?" He's sniggering at me now, the way he always does when he's gonna say something clever.

"History says it, Mitch. Grandma left Grandpa. Mom left Pops. She'd leave me. When she's back in L.A., things can just go back to how they were before. We stick to the plan."

Mitch laughs at me, and my eyes scold him with malice because I need to fucking know what he finds so amusing.

"What's funny?" I ask.

"You actin' like that ain't gonna hurt," he chuckles.

"I never said it wasn't gonna hurt, but I'm countin' on the

hope that not having to see her every day makes my life a lot easier, than it is now."

"And who says she has to leave?"

"You going senile? Did you not hear what I just said?"

"What I heard was bullshit. What I heard was you, comparing yourself to two other men. Yeah, your grandpa loved your grandma, and he lost her. He lost her because he fucked it up. Your father loved your mom, and we don't know what the hell went wrong with that, but knowing him, he probably fucked that up the way he did this place. What you're forgetting, Garrett, is that *neither* of those men are *you*. You see the real value in things, and you see the value in people."

He pulls open his shirt and shows the 'CR' that's branded on his chest.

"You think I still wear this for him?" His eyes shoot up to the rafter, where Grandpa hung himself.

"You think I stick around for a man who's dead?" he questions.

"I'm here for *you*. I believe in *you*. Don't be held back by history, son. Get out there and write your own." He stands up and buttons his shirt back up, then without waiting for a response, places his hat back on his head and heads out the door.

CHAPTER 20

MAISIE

"Do you know Leia?" I try making small talk with Garrett, when he drives me toward the Mayor's house. I'm really not looking forward to this party; it's the last thing I need. Garrett's barely spoken to me since the incident in his room, and tonight would have been the perfect opportunity to spend some time with him. I noticed the state of his hands, when he came back inside the house earlier, and when I offered to clean them up for him, he refused. I should have guessed he'd go back to avoiding me and being awkward.

"Wade knows her better than me, they're around the same age," he answers, pulling up outside the huge mansion-style home and cutting the engine.

"Looks fancy," I point out, looking at the elaborate, white, stone water fountain that's in the center of the driveway. I had no idea what to wear, and I wonder now, if I'm a little underdressed in the sweater dress I picked out.

"Call when you need pickin' up," Garrett practically growls at me, and I decide not to stand for it.

"You know, if I'm such an inconvenience, you could have

made Dalton, or Finn bring me here. You could have them pick me up, too," I point out, and it frustrates the shit out of me when he doesn't give me a response.

"I'm sure I could get a ride home with someone from here." I suggest, and without looking at me, he shakes his head like the idea pisses him off.

"Call me, and I'll come get you," he repeats, staring out the windshield.

"What if it's late?"

"I'll come get you." He still refuses to look at me.

"What if I'm wasted?" I decide he deserves to be taunted.

"I'll come get you," he tells me again, tensing his jaw and swallowing hard.

"What if it's late, and I'm wasted, and all I've been thinking about doing all night is kissing you?" I lean across the seat, and when he turns his head, he looks down at my lips like the thought tempts him.

"Then I'll come get you," he whispers softly, the same way he did when he was commanding me on his bed, earlier.

"Then I'll see you later," I smile sweetly, and before he can argue, I press a kiss on his cheek. The growl he makes, vibrates right in my chest, and when I pull away and open my door to get out, he says my name and makes me pause.

"You look real fucking pretty." His eyes glance over me, and I have to bite the smile from my lips as I slide out of the seat and slam the door.

Leia's party takes me by surprise. I never even knew there were these many young people in Fork River, and it's nowhere near as boring as I thought it would be. If the people here wore a little less clothes, it wouldn't be much different to the parties we have in L.A. I'm a popular attendee, due to the fact I'm new in town and everyone is nosy. And the more I drink, the more honest my answers to their questions become.

It takes a while but eventually, the hostess herself manages to find her way over to me; she wobbles as she tops my glass up with tequila, then stumbles as she sits down beside me. It's a little awkward that despite us never being introduced, she rests her head on my shoulder but, figuring the girl's wasted, I go with it.

"Is it true your mom's a gold digger who plans on taking all the Carson's money?" she asks, holding her head and closing her eyes like the room's spinning.

"I wouldn't put it past her," I shrug, before knocking back my shot and admiring the shock I just put on her face. That's a thing I find strange about most people, they seek the truth, but when they actually get it, it baffles them.

"And is it true that they gave you her room?" she asks, looking bewildered as she tries to coordinate placing the bottle on the coffee table.

"Who's room?"

"Breanna's," she leans in, and whispers behind her hand. "You know, the dead sister."

"No, I don't think so." I shake my head, feeling a little disturbed by the idea.

"No one saw it coming you know. She was best friends with my little sister, they told each other everything, and even she didn't see it coming,"

"What do you mean no one saw it coming. Was she in an accident?" I rack my brain, trying to figure it all out. No one ever talks about it, and considering it all happened so recently, I find it strange.

"God, no! Breanna killed herself. Just like her grandfather did. Well, not exactly like he did; she didn't hang herself. She jumped off Blackdrop Point. It's really pretty up there, especially in the fall. No one really ever goes up there anymore," she yawns sleepily.

I suddenly feel very fucking sober, and my heart breaks for Breanna, her brothers and Mr. Carson, too.

What a terrible way to lose a child.

"Did you know her?" I ask, wondering how much more I'm gonna get out of her. She looks like she's about to crash.

"Yeah, we used to hang out a little. Lottie noticed a change in her about a year before she died, she just detached herself from everything." Leia tells me lazily, then rests her head on the back of the couch and closes her eyes.

"That's really sad." I reach to the table and help myself to another tequila, downing it in one and trying to absorb everything I just heard. Garrett spoke to me about losing his grandfather, but he never mentioned that he'd lost Breanna in the same way. It must have been devastating for him.

"Are you ok?" I ask Leia, when she attempts to sit back up. Her eyes appear to have lost their focus.

"Yeah, I'm just dizzy. I've already called him..." she leans on my shoulder again, and taking out her cell, she clumsily scrolls down to the last number she called.

I'm a little shocked when I see Wade's name come up on the screen, and seeing as Leia seems to have lost the ability to speak, I take the phone out of her hand and wait for him to pick up.

"I'm on my way. I'll be five minutes, ok?"

"Wade, it's me, Maisie," I tell him.

"Maisie, where's Leia?" He sounds agitated and concerned, nothing like the guy I've gotten to know. "She's here with me, but she must have drank too much because she's kinda out of it."

"Shit! Maisie, listen to me. I need you to get her to the bathroom and make her throw up."

"Ewww... No way," I screw my face up at the thought of it.

"You remember that night me and Garrett took you to the bar, there were those three guys in the corner, and you asked me who they were? Are they there?" He sounds desperate, so I quickly scan the room and when I notice the meaner looking one, out of the three, standing by the patio doors, I speak up.

"Yes, I see one."

"Good, go give him the phone, so I can talk to him and get Leia to the bathroom. She needs to throw up, even if she acts like a brat about it."

I move fast and head toward the guy wearing an oversized tank top, he's got a harsh, unapproachable look on his face, but I haven't got time to let it put me off.

"Wade wants to talk to you." I thrust the phone at him, and his eyes peer down at me as he takes it. His thick, bottom lip, and the nose ring he wears, make him appealing and yet, he's not surrounded by female company. I guess that's due to the vibe he gives off.

I leave him with the phone and head straight back over to deal with Leia.

"Come on, we're going to the bathroom," I shake her awake, and when she barely stirs, I surprise myself with my own strength when I pull her up and start dragging her across the room.

"Lock the doors! No one fucking leaves!" I glance back over my shoulder when I hear the other guy from the bar shout out his orders. He's the one with longish, sandy blonde hair and shoulders like a ledge. The room comes to a standstill, but I keep moving, managing to get Leia into the bathroom, but when I lean her over the sink nothing happens.

"You need to throw up," I explain, and when she stares back at me dopily, I cringe at what I'm gonna have to do.

"Well, I guess this is one way of getting to know each other better." I blow out a breath before forcing my fingers into her mouth and reaching them to the back of her throat. Naturally, she struggles against me, but since she's wasted I'm stronger, and when I feel her start to heave, I retract my fingers and direct her back over the basin.

She throws up all over the shiny marble, coughing and spluttering as tears run down her cheeks.

"I'm so sorry." I hold back her hair, willing Wade to hurry

the fuck up. The door crashes open, and instead of Wade, the guy I gave the phone to, burst's inside.

"Leia, I still got Wade on the line. If you know who did this, I need a name." He stares her up and down, waiting for an answer, and just when I think Leia's too spaced to speak up, she wipes her hand over her mouth and her whole body trembles as she slides her back down the shower panel and sits her ass on the floor.

"Tyler," she manages, before she rolls her head and throws up on the floor.

"Tyler Phillips?" he checks, and when she nods her head, I see the sadness in her eyes.

"I liked him," she turns her head to me, and shrugs.

"Are you sure?" the guy checks.

"Yes, Noah, I'm sure." She presses her head back against the glass and breathes. "He got me alone in my room, and when I told him I wanted to go back down and enjoy the party, he got shitty with me. I haven't felt right since he got me that beer; it's why I called Wade. I always call Wade," she tells him, closing her eyes again.

I can't hear what Wade says to the guy on the phone, but it makes him rush off, leaving us alone together.

I try to keep Leia awake, by asking her questions. I've seen my fair share of drunk girls at parties. I'm usually one of them. But never like this. I hear a loud crash and a lot of commotion before Wade eventually thunders through the door.

"She thrown up?" he checks, looking worried, as he grabs Leia's face in his hand, and checks her over.

"Wade," she whispers his name, and he hugs her tight to his chest.

"It's ok, I'm here now. I'm here, darlin'." He closes his eyes and kisses the top of her head.

"I've got sick in my hair," she sobs.

"Yeah, darlin', you do. But it's alright, I'm gonna get you to bed, okay?"

"I don't want to go to bed. He'll be there, and I just wanna enjoy the party," she's slurring, and I can see the anger on Wade's face multiplying.

The door opens again, and the third guy I recognise from the bar interrupts us. He's dark-haired and has a tattoo, of what looks like a spider, on the side of his face.

"Noah's got him, found him down in the games room, fucking a girl in the same state she's in." His eyes glance over Leia while he waits on Wade's instruction.

"Tell Noah, I'll be there in a minute." Wade lifts Leia off the floor and starts carrying her out, and since I have no idea what to do with myself, I follow after him. He moves her effortlessly through the party and up the stairs, and when we get to Leia's bedroom, it's exactly how you'd expect the room of the Mayor's daughter to look. It's pretty and very pink, and Wade looks out of place in it as he lays her down on the bed. She snuggles her head into the pillow, and he stares down at her with every muscle in his body clenched.

"She's your curse, isn't she?" The words spill out of my mouth, and considering the mood he's in, I instantly regret them.

"She'll never know it." The way he looks at me, turns his words into a threat.

"Your secret's safe with me," I promise with a sad smile, and he nods gratefully before staring back at her.

"Stay with her." The fury finds his eyes again, and he starts making his way toward the door.

"Where are you going?" I call after him, but he's far too mad to answer.

I sit on the end of the bed and watch Leia sleeping, and suddenly I recall what the guy said to Wade. He caught Tyler, whoever he is, with a girl. One in the same state Leia's in.

Some poor girl at this party has been assaulted, and when I

hear all the chaos coming from outside, I move across to the window to see what's happening. Staring out onto the driveway, I see that the entire party has moved outside, and then I see Wade dragging a guy, who I assume to be Tyler, by the back of his shirt toward the fountain.

I watch through my fingers as he slams the back of the guy's head into the fancy, white stone.

Then twisting him around, he grabs the back of his neck and submerges him under the water.

I've never seen Wade look so angry; he's always the opposite of Garrett. Warm, friendly, and carefree. Not the man I'm watching hold Tyler's head under the water, in front of the crowd.

When he lifts him out, Tyler's desperate gasps for air prove that he's still alive, and I watch Wade mouth words tightly into his ear before he forces him back under again.

The three guys from the bar stand and watch, they stop Tyler's friends from intervening, and I hold my breath as I watch Wade physically drowning the guy in Mayor Walker's fountain.

The water that's illuminated by underwater lighting, turns red from the huge gash that's on Tyler's head, and there's no sign of Wade stopping.

"Where did you get it?" I hear him yell, as he lifts Tyler back out the water. People have their phones out recording him and seeing that this is about to go horribly wrong, I do the only thing I can think of, and call Garrett.

"You ready?" he answers on my first ring.

"Garrett, I need you to get here, now. I think Wade's gonna kill someone."

"You okay?" His voice instantly turns rigid.

"I'm fine, just get here quick." I check on Leia, and when I see she's breathing soundly, I rush down the stairs to try and talk some sense into Wade.

"Tell me now, where he got the shit or I swear to God, I

will bust his head apart!" Wade is screaming at Tyler's friend now, holding an unconscious, maybe even dead, Tyler by his hair.

"Wade." I step between him and the guy he's yelling at.

"Maisie, I told you to stay upstairs." He's furious, his chest rising and falling like a crazed psychopath, and when I see Garrett's truck pull up behind him, I don't have time to think about how he got here so fast, I'm just relieved to see him.

"Wade!" He calls out to his brother in that deep, commanding voice, and my stomach flips as he marches towards us and forces his brother to let Tyler go.

"Noah!" He calls one of the bar guys over and when the one with the nose ring steps up, "Handle crowd control, there's gotta be twenty fuckin' cell phones recording this shit." Garrett hisses through his teeth, as he holds Wade back from doing anymore damage.

"He dead?" He looks down at the dark-haired one, who's on the floor tending to Tyler.

"Got a pulse," he nods.

"Good, you take him back to Sawyer's place and ask Shelby to clean him up. Keep him there."

The guy gets straight to work and, with the help of the blonde one, hauls Tyler up, loads him into a Mercedes, and skids off.

"I'm gonna kill him, Garrett," Wade uses all his strength to push against him, but Garrett manages to hold him firm.

"Not here," the warning he whispers into his ear, sends a chill down my spine. And when Wade finally backs down, he scrubs his bloody hand over his face and picks up his hat from the floor.

"Son of a fucking bitch!" He kicks at the fountain with his boot, before resting his hands on his knees and steadying his breaths.

"Where's the girl, the one he was with when they found

him?" I ask, she must be scared, and if she's in as bad a state as Leia was, she'll need taking care of.

"I left her with one of her friends," Wade tells me, staring at the mess he's made of the fountain.

"What girl?" Garrett stares between us, confused.

"They found him down in the games room, he was…"

"Cunt," Garrett closes his eyes before looking over to Noah. He's got some kid pinned to the wall, by his neck, with one hand and is scrolling through his cell phone with the other.

"Noah," he calls out and grabs the guy's attention. "Ask your boss how he wants this handled, and if you need me, you know where to find me. No fucker does this shit in our town."

Noah nods his agreement, before he gets back to work.

"Come on. We're leaving," Garrett comes to stand beside me, and when his fingers slip between mine, I almost pull away in shock.

"We can't leave. What about Leia and the girl downstairs?"

"I got Leia," Wade assures me, and after what I've witnessed, I believe every word he says.

"And the girl?" I stare between both brothers, in shock.

"She'll be taken care of." Wade assures me of that, too, pulling himself together and heading toward the front door.

"Come on, let me take you home." Garrett starts leading me toward the truck, and I let him, looking around blankly at the shocked faces and devastation that's surrounding us. I get inside the truck when Garrett opens the passenger door for me, and mechanically I pull on my safety belt while Garrett moves around the hood to get behind the wheel.

"How did you get here so fast?" I ask, as he starts the engine. Suddenly I feel so drained, there are alot more important questions I could ask, but this is the one I want the answer to, now.

Garrett ignores my question and drives around the fountain, nodding his head to Noah as he passes him.

"And who are those guys? You talk to them like you do the bunkhouse boys." Again he ignores me,

"Garrett. How did you get here so fast? You arrived, like, five minutes after I called."

He breathes through his nostrils and stares at the road in front of him.

"Jesus, will you just fucking answer my question?" My body gets thrust forward, and I jolt back when the safety belt tightens from him slamming on the brakes.

"I told you about cursin', and why's it so fuckin' important how fast I fuckin' got here? I'm here, and that's all that matters." He looks at me like he's mad, that and the fact he's disregarding my questions makes me mad, too.

"It's important because I don't think you want to tell me the truth," I admit, fully aware of how bratty and stupid that sounds.

"You're right. I don't wanna tell ya." He focuses back on the road before he pulls back off, and that signals the end of our discussion.

CHAPTER 21

GARRETT

It's early morning when Wade gets back home, but I've been sitting on the porch, waiting for him for over an hour.

"You ever sleep?" he asks, slamming the door to his truck and joining me. He's got that boyish grin back on his face, so I figure all that red mist from last night has lifted.

"Not when there's work to be done," I tip the last of my coffee on the earthy ground and look at my brother.

"Noah called this morning, Tyler's badly hurt, but he's livin'."

"Not for long." Wade clicks his knuckles, quickly returning to being tense, and I can tell he ain't gonna let this lie.

"The River Boys questioned him when he came around, and you're not gonna believe where he got the shit from." I know what I'm about to tell Wade is only gonna fuel his anger. He's gonna want to act on it straight away, and I ain't even sure what kinda action we should take just yet.

"Try me." When he stares at me, I take a breath before I answer.

"Dear little Caleb Mason." I watch the shock drop on his face as I reveal that Ronnie's youngest son, and the apple of his eye, is behind all this.

"Caleb? Are you shittin' me?"

"No shit, turns out, Daddy's little hero is supplying the town's predators with Vetalar."

"Then I'm gonna kill him, too." Wade goes to stand up, but I pull him back down. "We gotta think about this, and before you think it, I ain't saying that we do nothin'. I'm suggesting we be smart and use this to our advantage."

"Garrett, the kid slipped that shit into Leia's drink. He was gonna rape her and let's not forget the fact he did rape the Woake's girl. He's gonna die, and anyone who helped him is gonna die, too."

"I agree, but what you're forgettin' is that you had a whole audience last night at that party. If he disappears now, everyone's gonna suspect it was you."

"So what are you suggestin'?" I can tell Wade ain't convinced, but he's prepared to listen, which is a start.

"I say you let him think he's got away with it. Have him show his face around town. He'll be shamed. No one likes a fuckin' rapist. He'll get a couple of hidings, too. The Woakes are well-liked people. Let the kid live in fear and watch him suffer until the day comes when you decide to put him out of his misery." My brother nods his head, like he sees the logic out of what I'm saying.

"And what about Caleb?"

"Caleb," I smile and light up a smoke. "We'll leave it to his Daddy to make his life hell. We're going to Mason, and we're gonna tell him what we know. We'll keep his secret and gain a little of the control we lost back. Mason is sitting nice and snug in Mayor Walker's pocket. I wonder how our Mayor would feel if he found out his daughter almost got raped by his main sponsor's son?"

"I'm not hearing anything in your story about me killin'

him." Wade frowns.

"There's better ways to ruin a man than to kill him."

"Oh yeah, how?" Wade laughs at me when I stand up.

"You let 'em live," I tell him simply, leaving him to think on that and heading back inside. I see Maisie loitering at the bottom of the stairs, and automatically my feet stop moving.

The fact I wouldn't answer any of her questions last night got her pissed at me, but I'd rather that than admit the truth. The truth is pathetic.

"Mornin'," I nod my head, as I pass her on my way to the dining room and take a plate from the buffet table where Josie has laid out breakfast. Maisie follows me, showing she's still angry when she snatches the plate, I offer her, out of my hand and seethes me with her eyes, as she loads it.

"Mornin' sis," Wade strolls in with a huge smile on his face. He's obviously thought on what I said and decided to go with it, and when he plants a kiss on Maisie's cheek, I swear if her hands weren't full, she'd slap him.

I take my space at the table and pour myself some juice. Maisie sits opposite me, still scowling, and when Wade joins us, an awkward silence fills the room.

"Are we gonna say grace too, you know, just to keep up this pathetic attempt we're making to be The Brady-fucking-Bunch?"

"Who the hell are the Brady Bunch?" Wade scoffs around his eggs, looking confused.

"It's an old TV show about two families coming together, through a second marriage. I'm surprised Maisie's heard of it." I add, just to really piss her off. I'm starting to take pleasure in her attitude. Sure, it makes me want to smash her into the wall and fuck the brat out of her, but knowing that she'd like me to, makes the suffering bearable.

"Re-runs, I used to watch them with my mother before she got dick-dizzy for your Pops." She answers back at me with a clever smile, that has me gripping my knife and fork tighter.

"Listen, can we not talk about Dad's dick over the breakfast table?" Wade places down his fork and slides his hand over his forehead.

"You're right. We should talk about what happened last night. When you nearly fucking killed someone." Maisie's focus turns to him, and he makes a real shit attempt to look sorry about it.

"I'm waiting?" her fingers tap impatiently on the table.

"You saw what he did; death wouldn't have been anything less than he deserved." Wade shrugs unapologetically.

"Jesus, when did I stop living with the Waltons and move in with the fucking Sopranos?" Maisie stands up and slams her palm on the table, and Wade stares at her with even more confusion.

"More old TV shows before your time." I glance across at him and explain, knowing that it will add to her frustration.

"Will you stop using old TV shows as references? It's pissing me off." Wade yells at her, and she's about to yell something back but holds her mouth open when Cole casually strolls into the room, loads himself up a plate and sits at his space at the table.

Everyone stops to stare at him, and it takes him a while to notice since he's so busy tucking in.

"What?" he looks up innocently. "I heard Pops and his trophy wife were away, and breakfast in the Mason's bunkhouse tastes like it's been through a rat's ass." He continues to dig in, and Maisie shakes her head in disbelief.

"You know what? I'm done trying to figure this shit show out. The sooner I leave for home, the better." Her chair scrapes the floor before she strops out, and I hate how much those words hurt.

"Jeez, she really is a bitch, ain't she? Can you pass the salt?" Cole looks up to Wade, who, I guess, gives up trying to figure him out and slides it over with a hard shove.

CHAPTER 22

MAISIE

I go outside to the stables to find Dalton, but instead I find one of the other bunkhouse boys. "Ma'am," he lifts off his hat and smiles at me playfully.

"Where's Dalton?" I ask, searching around for him.

"Day off. Name's Tate," He extends his hand to me, and when I take it, his strong grip almost crushes my bones.

"I need you to give me a ride to the Mayor's house," I order, and when he raises his eyebrows at me, I realize I may have spoken a little too harshly.

"Please," I add, none of this is his fault. I just hate being kept in the dark. Wade was gonna kill that boy last night, I saw it in his eyes, and today he's cracking jokes. Even Garrett seemed in a good mood, and he's never in a good mood. I need answers, and since Leia Walker is now the closest thing I have to a friend in this weird-as-fuck town, it's her that I'm gonna go to.

"Well, since you asked so nicely…" he shakes his head and laughs to himself as he passes me and steps out onto the yard. I follow him, and get into the passenger seat of the truck he climbs into.

Tate drops me off at the gates, and after he drives off, I realize I probably should have asked him to wait. I tried calling Leia on the way over here, but she didn't pick up, and when I walk past the staff ,who are scrubbing the blood off the fountain, to knock on the door, I hope she's in.

The door opens, and I'm taken off guard by the 6ft tall silver fox, who answers it.

"Mr. Mayor," I drop my knee to curtsey, and instantly feel foolish when I realize that isn't his actual name.

"Maisie Wildman," knitting his brows together, he studies me hard. "I remember you from the wedding." He opens the door wider so I can step inside. "Your mother said you would probably be calling around. Glad to see you're settling in." I look over my shoulder at the fountain and wonder if he's going to mention it.

"Leia," he calls out for his daughter, and when she appears from the living room she looks nothing like I expected her to. I imagined she'd be a mess; almost being raped is a big deal, and I can't imagine her head's feeling all that clear either. Yet she stands in front of me, dressed in a blue dress that finishes respectively at her knees, with her hair pinned up in a pleat.

"I'll leave you girls to it. We leave in ten, sweetheart," he reminds her, stepping away into the room I guess is his office.

"What the hell?" I grab her by her arm and drag her into the living room. "Are you ok?" Searching her over, I look for any evidence of last night's trauma. I'm really starting to think I imagined it.

"Of course I'm not ok," her eyes fill up with tears and as sad as it is, I can't help feeling relieved that I'm not going crazy.

"Does he know?" I look over my shoulder, toward her father's office.

"Yeah, Wade and him talked before he left here this morning."

"Wait, Wade stayed here last night?" I don't why I'm so shocked by that. Wade was never gonna leave her.

"He slept on the floor. We're just friends." She passes it off as no big deal, but I know that, to Wade, it's much more than that.

"Do you know what happened to Tyler?" I ask.

"I was gonna ask you the same thing. I take it from the state of outside that Wade got to him?"

"Wade nearly killed him. Garrett had him taken somewhere by those guys with the tattoos."

"Noah," she corrects me.

"No, not him, he stayed behind. The other two took him."

"That'll be Sawyer and Zayne."

"Yeah, about them, who the hell are they? Garrett and Wade seem to have some kind of control over them."

"They don't control them. No one controls the River Boys," she shakes her head.

"The River Boys, that's what they call themselves?" I try not to laugh. What the hell is this place?

"No, people call them that, and no one fucks with them. Not even your brothers. They just all seem to have a mutual respect for each other."

"They're not my brothers," I snap. If they were, it would make the fact I constantly think about Garrett's hands on me, really wrong.

"Whatever, all you need to know is that Wade won't be in any trouble," she assures me, and when I hear footsteps come from behind me, I turn around and face Mr. Walker.

"Maisie, will you be riding with us to church?" He buttons up his suit jacket and looks up at me, expectantly.

"Church?"

"Of course she's coming with us, Daddy," Leia answers for me, linking her arm to mine and smiling sweetly. He turns around and heads for the door, and she leans in a little closer. "If I'm going down, you're coming with me," she smiles.

Mr. Walker makes polite conversation as he drives us to church and yet there is still no mention of what happened last night. I'm really not dressed for church. Ripped jeans and a top that shows off half my midriff hardly seem appropriate, but when we pull up at the chapel and head inside, I figure it's too late to worry about that.

Mr. Walker opens the door for me and flashes me a handsome smile before I step into the chapel, and I'm surprised to see that it's full. Who knew that the people of Fork River were so religious? I follow Leia up the aisle, straight to the front, and when I glance to my left and see all three Carson brothers sitting on the opposite pew, my knees almost buckle with shock.

Garrett does a double-take when he sees me and keeps a stern look on his face as he focuses back at the priest, standing at the altar.

I never had the Carsons down as religious men, and throughout the whole service I feel him side-glancing at me. When the organ starts to play, Wade sings loud and unashamedly, without the need of a hymn book. While Cole and Garrett's lips barely move, and I take it all in, wondering how everyone can act so normal.

After the service is over everyone congregates on the lawn outside, and I watch all three Carsons step out of the church doors, and place their hats back on their heads. Cole takes off first, heading to where his truck is parked on the other side of the street, while Wade and Garrett make a beeline toward us.

"Mayor Walker," Wade lifts his hat, like he's seeing him for the first time today, and I want to scream. Garrett must sense it because he wraps his hand around my arm and pulls me tighter to his body.

"We best be on our way," he excuses us, and despite wanting to protest, I don't pull away.

"Tell your father I said hello." Mayor Walker nods at Garrett, before looking at me. "And to your mother, of course." I wonder if she's already lined him up to be her next victim. He's younger than Bill, presumably richer, and he holds a much higher status. I know Leia has a mother. I saw her at the wedding, but I haven't seen any signs of her since. My mother's never let a simple problem, like a wife, stop her before.

I play my part in this little charade and smile back at him.

"Of course, and thank you for the ride." I nod politely and let Garrett lead me away.

When we get to Garrett's truck he opens the door for me, and I can tell by the way he slams it shut once I'm in, that he's pissed.

"What the *fuck* were you thinkin', leaving the ranch without tellin' me?" He growls, once he's in the driver's seat. I can sense the heat coming off him, and I know I shouldn't make him any angrier but, fuck it.

"Oh, I'm sorry, I thought we lived under the premise of *not* telling each other what's going on," I bite back sarcastically. "How about you tell me what the hell happened last night, and then we can get on to the subject of why I need your permission to do anything?"

"You were there, you saw what happened," he says impatiently.

"I saw Wade nearly kill someone." The fact he isn't seeing that as a big deal scares me.

"Yeah, well that weren't anythin' that someone didn't deserve." Garrett can't look me in the eye.

"Is he… dead?" I question, wondering if that's the reason why.

"No, the River Boys took care of it."

"The River Boys, and what exactly is it that the *River Boys* do?" I cross my arms and wait for an explanation.

"They do what they're told," he shrugs, and I try my best not to be distracted by how hot he looks driving and focus on what's important.

"See, I've heard different. I heard that..."

"It's a small town, you're gonna hear a lot, but that don't mean it's the truth." He cuts me off. And then comes the silence.

"How did you get there so fast?" I ask the same question I did last night. The one he avoided, and when he slows down and pulls over, he looks really pissed off that I'm asking him again.

"Does it really fuckin' matter?" He shakes his head at me, like I'm exhausting him.

"Yes." I stare right back, he's as handsome as he is intimidating, and I can't help wondering if he'll give in to what we have between us, before I leave for L.A.

"I got there fast..." he closes his eyes, and for a second, I don't think he's gonna finish.

"I got there fast... because I never left," his nostrils flare, and his forehead furrows, like he's mad at himself.

"That makes no sense."

"I parked around the corner because I wanted to be close just in case anythin' happened, which it turns out, was a pretty good fuckin' call,"

"Why?" It's a simple question, but it seems a hopeless one. I already know he's not gonna give me an honest answer.

"Because... because I care. Alright, ya happy now? What happened to her could have happened to you, and the thought of that..."

"Thank you." I put him out of his misery when I see him struggling, and reaching across the seat between us, I take his hand in mine and bring it to my lips. Slowly I kiss his rough, broken knuckles, and he closes his eyes again like I'm causing him pain, rather than showing tenderness.

"The River Boys do the Mayor's dirty work, and sometimes our paths cross. We have a shared interest in this town, and when it comes to lowlife's like Tyler Phillips, we help each other out. There's a history between us, and they respect it."

"Ok," I don't press him for more because I sense what he's just told me has cost him enough pride, but as he turns his head and re-starts the engine, I promise myself that I'll find out what that history is.

"So church, huh?" I feel the smirk pull on my face as he pulls back onto the road,

"It's good to keep up appearances," he points out.

"A Mayor who needs three hot guys to do his dirty work, turning up to church on a Sunday, all seems a little corrupt to me."

"Darlin', this whole town's corrupt." Garrett lets out a deep-throated laugh, and the half smile he makes, has my stomach doing that weird, flippy thing again.

CHAPTER 23

GARRETT

"You gotta promise me you're gonna keep your cool," I warn Wade, as we stare outta the windshield at the Mason's gate. I know how mad he is about what happened to Leia Walker, and my brother's had a thing for her for as long as I can remember, but he's barking up the wrong tree with that one. She's never gonna lower her standards to a cowboy, it don't matter how big his ranch or his fortune is.

"We'll just see how he responds. If he starts making excuses for him, I don't know if I can be good on that promise, bro." Wade warns, and I take a deep breath before I drive through the gates.

It's been a while since I've been here. I never bother to attend any of the parties Ronnie Mason puts on as an excuse to brag to the folk in town, and looking around, I can see the place has developed a lot since I last visited.

Our ranch used to be the town's sole supplier; no one could touch us. We branched out all over the state, but these days we can't compete. If it weren't for all the family money that we still have, invested from the days when our great, great grandad mined the Ridge, we would have probably gone under last winter.

There's more than enough of it left for us to live on, but that ain't how the Carsons, that came before us, built their legacy.

They worked hard, so they had something to pass on. I see no pride in taking a dead man's money and failing with it. And I vowed last year that we would never see another winter the same. No matter how underhanded I have to be.

Pops sees getting his government seat as more important than our future here, and I see things differently.

We get some dodgy looks from the bunkhouse boys when we pull up in the yard, and me and Wade stare 'em right back as we get out the truck.

"We're here to speak with your boss," I call out, to no one in particular.

"He'll be inside," one of them speaks up, and I recognise Seth, who I sacked a few weeks ago, now wearing the Mason shirt, as he gestures his head toward the main house. He's irrelevant to me now, so I don't give him the courtesy of a response as I head in that direction.

The Mason home is modern; its glass front and shiny steel frame look intrusive against the beautiful valleys behind it. I move toward the front door with Wade behind me, noting that I saw no sign of Cole in the yard. He probably made sure of that because he knew we were coming. He'll already be getting the shit pulled out of him because of who he is, and where he's come from. Us being here, will only be a reminder of that.

I tap my knuckles at the door, and when a pretty brunette answers, I give her one of my more friendly smiles.

"We're here to see Mr. Mason," I tell her,

"Which one? There are five of 'em," she tries being smart with me.

"Senior," I inform her, before looking back at Wade. He's already breathing like an ox, there ain't no way he's gonna keep his cool, and I hope and pray that Caleb Mason ain't anywhere near because, right now, Wade wants to make someone hurt.

"Come in, I'll get him for you." She opens the door wider and shows us to the bench seat in the hall. Everything here is so urban; it's like someone picked up a New York penthouse and dumped it in the middle of the plains. Nothing about this structure belongs here, especially the people living in it.

Neither of us takes a seat, we remain standing while we wait, and when the decrepit, old man hobbles out of his office, relying on his stick, I understand why he doesn't seem to have much of a presence around town, anymore.

"You boys here for work, too?" He laughs to himself, and when Wade moves to step forward, I hold out my arm to block him.

"No, sir. We're actually here with some information that I think you might find useful." I step closer to him myself, making sure I tower over his hunched frame.

"Leia Walker was drugged at a party last night," I start off, feeling the tension coming from Wade beside me. "Another girl was drugged and raped,"

"What is the world coming to?" Old man Mason shakes his head but doesn't look much like he cares.

He will.

"We spoke to the kid responsible," I assure him.

"And I hope that all those extra taxes I've been paying, ensure he's reprimanded for it," he looks up at me, unfazed.

"He told us where he got his supply." Knowing I'm about to ruin this fucker's day helps me stay calm.

"What ya here to do, Garrett, round up a posse?" The bastard laughs again, and now I really do have to hold Wade back.

I turn my body into his and warn him with my eyes. I've never met anyone as laid back as Wade, but when he's loaded like he is now, there ain't no reasoning with him.

"Cool it," I warn him, through my teeth.

"Would you be cool if it was Maisie who got drugged?" he asks, raising his eyebrows, and when I decide I have no argument back to that, I turn back around to face Ronnie Mason.

"Your son, Caleb, he's a vet, right?" I narrow my eyes at him.

"Opening his own practice in town next spring," he smiles proudly.

"So he has easy access to drugs, like Vetalar?" I let him know where I'm going with this.

"I don't know what you're suggesting, but…"

"I ain't suggestin' anything. I'm *tellin'* ya. Your son's supplying these predators. He's putting that stuff out on our streets, and if Mayor Walker found out that it was *your* son who put *his* daughter in that situation, I think he might want to re-evaluate your relationship."

It's not a secret that the Mason's success wasn't just built by their fortune. They also relied on a lot of influential power. I step even closer to him, keeping hold of his stare.

"You know, before you came to town, ranchers around here looked out for each other. So, I'm gonna give ya a little taste of how it used to be. I'll keep your secret. I'll rely on the hope that you're a good enough man to teach that boy of yours a lesson of your own. Because I don't know what you've heard, but I can assure you, he wouldn't want to learn that lesson from us,"

I turn to walk away, noticing how Wade ain't budging.

"I've heard a lot about how this town was run before I came to it. Apparently, Carsons used to brand men like slaves." His words have me turning on my feet and staring back at him.

"Then you heard wrong. Branded men were free men. They protected our ranch, and they protected each other. They took the brand out of loyalty. Maybe if you had some of that, you'd understand them better." I put him right.

"But mainly, they protect you, right?" He has a pretty, smug smile on his face for someone who just found out his son's a drug-supplying cunt. I head straight for him and grip him by the fancy jacket he's wearing, and just like my father, he looks much more like a politician than a ranch owner.

He gasps in shock when I shove him into the wall and lift him up off his feeble feet.

"Do I look much like I need protecting?" I ask, and when he doesn't answer, I let him drop to the floor like a bag of bones, and along with my brother, I head back out the door.

Wade doesn't have much to say on the way home, and he heads straight out to the stables when we pull up at the ranch. There's a mustang Pops had Tate and Finn round-up yesterday; apparently, the thing's bat-shit crazy. I guess he's gonna throw himself around on that to let off some steam.

I head inside, and when I find Maisie lying on the couch talking on her cell, I hang up my hat and head into the kitchen. I grip the basin and restrain myself from ripping it from the damn wall. She seems to be everywhere. In my space. In my thoughts. I can still taste her on my tongue, and I can't close my eyes without seeing her smiling back at me.

"I was talking to Leia. She invited me back over, tomorrow night," Maisie mentions casually as she steps around me and grabs herself an apple from the fruit bowl. She hops herself up onto the kitchen work surface beside me, and sinks her teeth into it.

"I'm bored. You wanna hang out? Maybe we could take another shower?" She's taunting me, and I feel my cock stiffen under my jeans. I wish I didn't care enough about her, to stop myself from doing all things I've thought about. And like always, the girl knows exactly how to make me lose control.

I shift my body, so my hips rest between her open thighs. It would be so easy to take her like this. To allow myself everything I've desired since she first stropped onto my porch and started fuckin' with my head.

Placing my palms flat on the work surface either side of her hips and pressing my forehead into hers, I decide to give her a taste of her own medicine.

"I warned you 'bout teasin'," I growl, letting my cock press between her legs.

"You did, but I suck at doing as I'm told. I like teasing you. I like making you mad. What ya gonna do about it?" She shrugs her shoulders, then gasps when I snatch her jaw in the arch of my hand and squeeze. I look down at her lips and admire the way I've pursed them together. It's hard not to imagine how pretty they'd look with me feeding my cock through them, and I can't help wondering if she'd manage to take me all the way to the back of her throat. I'm sure I'd like the sound of her gagging just as much as I do her laughter.

"I ain't gonna do nothin'," I assure her. The only justice in my torture is the fact she suffers it ,too. I'm a cruel-hearted man for having those kinda thoughts, but it's the only pain I ever want her to feel, and for that reason, I can't keep Maisie Wildman. I have to set her free.

I drop my hand from her jaw and turn away, heading out the door and getting as far away from her as I can manage.

"You're a coward, Garrett Carson!" she calls out after me, and I don't turn around to see if she's smiling or pouting. I also don't correct her. I could drag her to watch me kill a hundred men to prove to her that I ain't. But when it comes to her, she's right. I'm a fucking coward.

CHAPTER 24

MAISIE

"You look beautiful." Bill kisses Mom on her cheek, as she grabs her raincoat from the hook. She's going out for dinner with a bunch of women from the flower-arranging club she's joined. Considering I've never seen my mom arrange a flower in her life, and the fact I don't even think she likes them, I'm assuming that another member of the club holds some kind of stature she wants to associate with.

"Are you sure you don't want one of the boys to drive you? That storm's coming in pretty heavy," he checks.

"I'm fine, and you don't want them waiting around for me," she refuses.

"Well then, drive safe," Bill warns her, handing over the keys to his truck.

"I'll be back before eleven," she promises, heading for the door.

"You're out with Leia tonight aren't you, darling?" Mom's overjoyed at how close we've come since the party. Another connection she can use for her benefit, I guess.

"Yeah, her parents are out of town, so we're just gonna chill at her place," I answer. "I was gonna see if I can catch a ride."

"Darling, I'm going in the opposite direction. Have one of the boys take you. That's what you pay them for isn't it, darling?" She looks at Bill, and the dopey smile he gives her back makes me want to vomit.

"I'll have Dalton take you," he agrees, taking out his cell and making the call.

Mom kisses his cheek and dashes off, and just as Bill hangs up from giving his orders, my phone vibrates in my pocket.

I read Leia's message and feel a little disappointed.

"Cancel that ride," I tell Bill. "Leia is staying in Billings for the night, and her Dad doesn't want her driving back in the storm,"

Bill nods his head, before calling Dalton back.

"Just me and you then," he smiles at me a little awkwardly when he puts his cell back into his pocket. Unfortunately, he's right. Wade's away in Tulsa, and Garrett's avoiding me like I have an incurable disease. He left for camp four days ago and hasn't been back since. He didn't even return with the cowboys earlier today, after they rounded up some of the herd and brought them into the huge outhouse to protect them from the storm.

I only have a week before I leave for college, and feel like he's stealing time away from me.

"You wanna watch a movie?" Bill at least tries to make the effort, and since I got nothing better to do, I agree.

Thirty minutes into the film I'm already regretting letting him choose what we watch, and I keep my eye on the door, watching and willing for Garrett to walk through it.

I notice Bill frowns with disappointment as he reads the message that comes through on his phone.

"That was your mother. She's staying at Denise's. It's getting bad out there." Placing his phone back on the armrest, he fidgets uncomfortably in his chair.

I wonder if he suspects that she's cheating on him. It never usually takes her very long to set to work on her next prospect, and I'm certainly not buying her story about staying at Denise's place.

I can already hear the wind whipping around the house, and I can't help worrying that Garrett is still out there.

I manage to make it through to the end of the movie, and when the credits start to roll, I fake a yawn so I can take myself to bed.

"I should head up," I tell him, dragging myself off the couch.

"Goodnight, Maisie." Bill nods his head at me, before I make my way up the stairs.

When I get to my room I look out of my window toward the bunkhouse. The lights are on, and I can just about hear the music traveling across the yard through the wind and rain. I guess all the wranglers are in there, rewarding themselves after a hard day. I know bringing the herd in would have taken a lot of work, and there was a lot of panic when the weather warning came in this morning. I just hope Garrett is in there with them. I've spoken a little to Leia over the past few days about how I feel for him, and she wasn't judgy. In fact she offered some pretty sound advice. Not that I can take it. To talk to him about our situation would involve him having to be around.

I've also come to the conclusion that she is completely oblivious to the fact that Wade is in love with her. She's got the poor guy friend-zoned, and the way she's been talking about Caleb Mason, suggests he's got no way out of it.

I get myself tucked into bed and start reading the book she lent me a few days ago, and when my eyes start to feel heavy, I give up and let them close.

A loud smash startles me out of my sleep, and when I hear some rustling downstairs I sit up. Another crashing noise comes, and I spring up on my feet wondering if it might be Garrett. Maybe he got a little drunk at the party they had in the bunkhouse. I'd like to see Garrett drunk. He's always so serious and controlled. Maybe the conversation I need to have with him would be easier if he were a little wasted.

I creep on to the landing and peek over the banister, but there's nobody there. The noises seem to be coming from Bill's office, and hearing the loud whispers and more rustling, has me heading down the stairs so I can see what's going on.

The scene I walk in on makes my heart jump into my throat. I see four men, all dressed in black and wearing ski masks, three of them are turning the office upside down looking for something, and a fourth man stands pointing a gun at Bill. Bill sees me before they do, and he discreetly shakes his head at me. It's a warning, he's telling me to run, but it's too late; before I can move, I feel someone clutch at my arm.

"What do I do with this one?" his voice comes out muffled, through the mask.

"Shit," the guy holding the gun lowers his arm,

"Get her in the corner." He raises it back up, pointing it at me to ensure I do what he says and I get dragged, by the guy bruising my arm, into the corner and forced to sit on my ass.

Bill's white as sheet, and I can tell from the way he's trembling that he's scared.

"Just tell us where it is, and we'll go. No one has to get hurt, here." The one holding the gun speaks, and when the man who's pulling apart the bookshelf stops and crosses the room, something catches my eye.

It's a belt buckle, like the ones Garrett has in his room and similar to the one Wade won at the rodeo a few weeks ago. This one I remember because it was unique, and I know who it belongs to.

"I got something," he holds up a brown file, and when the men start to back away, I feel myself breathe a sigh of relief. I watch the guy with the buckle tuck the file into the front of his pants, then pull his hoodie over it, and when he comes closer he crouches in front of me.

"If only I had more time," his gloved hand slides through my hair. "I'd enjoy making a mess out of you." He lifts up his mask just enough to expose his mouth, and when I feel his tongue slide over my cheek, I gag.

He stands up and moves out, like the others, and I sit and wait until the door slams before I scramble across the floor to get to Bill. He's not white anymore, in fact, his skin's turned purple, and he's clutching at his arm like he's been shot. When I hear tires screech out the yard, I quickly rush to the window to get a look at the car they drove away in.

A bullet wound in the arm can wait, Mom's first husband was Chief of Police, and he'd drum into me how important it was to take in all the details if I ever found myself involved in a crime. Maybe that's the reason I recognised Jason's buckle. I watch the black sedan speed off down the track and just manage to catch the license plate before it gets out of sight.

Bill's moans distract me as I jot the number down on a pad on his desk. He's trying to tell me something, and when I start trying to tend to him and see no blood, I try to recall hearing the gun go off, but I can't, and as his face creases in agony, I realize that this isn't a bullet wound, it's a heart attack. Rushing to the desk, I pick up the phone to dial 911.

I'm screaming at the operator, begging them to hurry, when Garrett races into the room. He looks mad and panicked all at the same time when he sees his dad laying on the floor.

"What happened?" he rushes toward him and drops to his knees, checking his father over, and I notice that Bill's stopped making any sound. He's not moving, and when Garrett starts frantically pumping at his chest, I scream at the operator for them to hurry again.

Mitch is the next one in, and when he sees what's happening he immediately takes over from Garrett.

"What happened?" I drop the phone when Garrett grabs both my arms and holds me firm. At first, I have no words because I don't know what just happened.

"Jason," the name spills out of my lips, and when I see the anger on Garrett's face turn to confusion, I figure I'm gonna have to do better.

"Him and some others, they were looking for something, and I thought he was shot, but… is he alive?" I look down to where Mitch is still pumping at Bill's chest and sob.

"Maisie, listen to me. Who else was here?"

"I don't know, they drove away a few minutes ago, a black sedan," I shrug myself free from his hold and grab the license plate number off the desk.

Mitch is still trying to resuscitate Bill, but the sad shake of his head tells us both that he's not coming back.

"I'm sorry," I burst into more tears, and when I look back at Garrett, instead of his tears I see pure, murderous rage looking back at me. His nostrils flare and his chest heaves, and the stare he makes at the body of his father tells me exactly what he's gonna do next.

I tug on his arm when he starts moving. He can't go after them, there's too many, and they're armed. I can't let him leave.

"Garrett, please," I beg, but he rips his arm from my hand and moves toward the cabinet in the corner of the room. He takes out a rifle and a box of ammo, and it spills out all over the desk when he loads up the barrels.

"Please, the ambulance is on its way. We know who one of them is. The police can deal with this." My words don't seem to be registering as he cocks the gun and fills his pockets with more ammo.

"I'm scared. Please don't go after them," I cry, and when he steps towards me, I don't know whether to be shocked or relieved when he reaches his hand around the back of my head and pulls me towards him. He grips at my hair, and his lips press into the top of my head so hard I feel them trembling.

"Mitch is gonna take care of you," he promises, keeping his lips tight to my head. "You have no reason to be scared, " he whispers, and when he releases me, heading for the door, I feel my heart break as I helplessly watch him leave.

CHAPTER 25

GARRETT

I throw the rifle on to the passenger seat, and get behind the wheel. My blood is pumping more adrenaline into my veins that I can cope with, and my sweaty palms clutch the wheel as I swing the truck into reverse and race off after the men who just killed my father. I have to remind myself to breathe as I speed down the open road, and when I realize I have no idea where I'm headed, I reach into my pocket and pull out my cell.

"What's up?" Noah yells, over the loud music in the background.

"I'm sending you a license plate number," I tell him, taking my phone away from my ear so I can type it into my messages.

"Have Zayne figure out who it belongs to and get right back to me,"

"Is it urgent? Zayne's a little…"

"Yeah, its fuckin' urgent," I snap at him impatiently.

"Yo, Zayne…" I hear Noah call out, over the loud music. "Dust off ya nose. I need ya,"

"What's this about, Garrett?" Noah comes back to me sounding serious.

"My father's dead." Saying the words out loud makes me feel sick. I've spent years butting heads with my old man. Wishing he'd step down and let me take over running the ranch.

Suddenly, none of that seems important. What matters is the fact he was at every single one of my football games, he taught me how to spot a decent bull at an auction, and that he was there to hold us all while we cried when Mom abandoned us.

As I stare out the windshield, the rain's coming down so hard I can barely see anything in front of me, and when I hear Noah's voice again, I remember he's still on the line.

"Your plates are registered to a Danny Holston. Grylls Creek Ranch. You know it?"

"Yeah, I know it," I recall the name, too. The small ranch between here and Columbus stopped functioning a few years back. Danny came to the ranch looking for work. I'd heard some rumors about him being thrifty, so I didn't take him on.

"You need some backup?" Noah checks. The kid always seems thirsty for a fight.

"Get back to your party," I hang up the phone and clench the wheel tight in my fists, then taking the road that leads to Columbus, I head for Grylls Creek.

I think of Maisie and how scared she looked when I left. I can't let myself feel bad for leaving her, not while I'm carrying all this anger. Right now, she needs reassurance and comfort, and I can't offer her that.

I pull up a safe distance from the derelict ranch, and when I see the sedan parked up outside the house and notice a light on inside, I feel a rush of relief. My phone rings for what has to be the twentieth time, and I give in and pick it up.

"Garrett, what the fuck's happened?" Cole yells down the line at me.

"He's dead, and I'm gonna make 'em dead, too," I tell him blankly as I stare at the house in front of me.

"I'm at the ranch; where are you?" he asks, sounding worried.

"Have you spoken to Wade?" Through the window I see two men sitting on the couch while another walks in front of the window, talking on the phone.

"Yeah, he's trying to get a flight back from Tulsa, but they've stopped all flights 'cause of the storm... Garrett, tell me where you are. I'll get to you."

"Take care of Maisie, she's scared," I tell him, hanging up the phone and sliding on my leather gloves before I pick up the rifle.

I trudge across the yard toward the front door and let myself in without hesitation. The three men are kicking back with a beer, and if it weren't for the three masks, the envelope of cash and the gun on the coffee table, I'd think I was in the wrong house.

"Fuck!" One of them quickly reaches for the gun, and I blow a hole into his arm and send him to the ground. I cock the lever to reload, before I pick up the handgun myself and check if it's loaded.

"Don't see many semi-automatics around here." I study it before pointing it at the two men sitting on the couch.

"Where's Jason?" I press my boot into the throat of the man on the floor, and both of the fuckers who were brave enough to invade my home stare back at me in fear.

"Come on, speak up. Where is he?" Both flick their eyes between me and their friend.

"He took off,"

"I wanna know where he took off to, and I wanna know what was important enough for you to break into my home and kill my father for. Because whatever it was, you better hope it was worth dying for,"

"We didn't kill nobody. Nobody got hurt," The one with the ponytail shakes his head in confusion, and I use the semi-automatic in my hand to shoot him right between his eyes. Blood splatters all over his friend, and I watch him turn pale as it dawns on him how much shit he's in.

"First thing you should know about me is, I don't tolerate fucking lies," I tuck the handgun into the back of my jeans and use the barrel of the rifle in my other hand to force the guy on the floor's mouth open.

"What's your name?" I turn my attention back to the guy on the couch.

"Holson," his voice quakes.

"You ever seen anyone get their head blown off, Holson?" I sound calm, but on the inside I feel my pulse beating in my ears.

"No, sir," he shakes his head frantically, as the man with my barrel between his lips makes a terrified moan.

"I need you to tell me where Jason is, and I need you to tell me what he took from me,"

"I don't know where he is, and I swear that's the truth. That cash, right there." His eyes flick to the money on the table. "That's all we got out of it, and it wasn't taken from your place. Nothing was taken from your place but the file. This was just a job for us. Jason was the one who set it all up,"

"What file?" I push my barrel deeper, making the guy on the floor choke.

"Some details for an off-shore account. That's all I know," The bastard's crying now, and I can only guess it's because he's out of information.

"Did you touch the girl?" I think about the way Jason looked at her that night in the bar before I knocked his ass out. This has got revenge written all over it. I made a fool of him, and this is his retaliation. The guilt of that makes my guts twist, and the anger inside me multiplies.

I swear if any of these assholes, left alive, have touched her, I'll make their death a long, drawn out fucking process.

"She wasn't touched. And I don't know what happened with

the old man, but no one was supposed to get hurt," he shakes his head desperately.

"Well, you really fucked up on that one, Holson," I pull my trigger, and the guy on the floor's head explodes. Blood and brains decorate the walls, and splatter on my skin, while Holson throws up all over the carpet.

I carefully step across the floor and drag a still gagging, Holson onto his feet, placing the rifle in his trembling hands.

"You ever fired one of these before?" I ask, cocking the lever for him and pointing it at the headless body on the floor.

"Once or twice," he swallows thickly as I place his finger over the trigger and press the semi-automatic against his temple. He's shaking like a shitting dog, and when I pull back his finger and the thing goes off, he screams in terror and drops it to the floor.

He's hysterical, completely lost it, and I step in front of him and pull the trigger on the semi-automatic I'm holding. Firing it into his head, I put him out of his misery, and I watch his body fall sideways and smash through the glass table. I place the handgun in the good hand of the other guy. Then taking one final look around at the massacre, I make sure all traces of me being here are gone, and step back out the door.

Three down, one to go.

CHAPTER 26

MAISIE

It's been hours since Garrett left. The ambulance has been, and since there was nothing they could do for Bill, they've taken him to the mortuary. Mitch called Mom to break the news, and instead of taking him up on his offer to pick her up, she refused. Apparently, she needs to be among friends. Friends, she's known for a matter of weeks. Not her daughter, who was just held at gunpoint and just watched her stepfather die. It hurts that she has no desire to comfort me, but it doesn't come as a surprise. My mother has always been good at putting herself first.

"Can you try calling him again?" I ask Mitch, when he hands me a whiskey. The liquid swishes in the glass from how much my hands are shaking, and no matter how hard I focus, I can't make it stop.

"Cole's out looking for him. He'll find him," he tries to reassure me, but it doesn't work. I saw how savage he was when he left here. He had every intention of making those men suffer.

"You should go to bed. It's late,"

"I can't. The police might come and they'll need to speak to me."

"They won't be here till morning, not in this storm," Mitch tells me.

He's probably right; it's got even worse out there in the last hour, which makes me even more concerned about Garrett.

"I'll sleep in Cole's old room so you won't be here alone. You need to rest," he orders, and when I down what's left in my glass and stand up, I pull the blanket that he wrapped around my shoulders earlier, a little tighter.

The rain's beating hard against the windows, the thunder's still crashing, and every now and then the whole house flashes blue.

"He shouldn't be out there in this, especially when he's so mad," I stare outside and think about where he might be now, or worse, what those men could be doing to him.

"Garrett will be just fine," Mitch's low gravelly voice soothes me, as he leads me toward the stairs. "I'll wake ya if there's anything to tell,"

I'm about to do what Mitch says, but when his phone rings, I pause in case it's an update.

"It's Cole," he tells me before answering, and I try hard to hear what he's saying. It's too muffled, but judging from the look on Mitch's face, it's not good.

"What is it? Where is he?" Tears stream from my eyes, and more panic starts to build in my chest when Mitch hangs up the phone and slams his fist into the banister.

"Damn it," he growls, scrubbing both hands over his face in frustration.

"Mitch, tell me right now what's happened,"

"Garrett just walked into a bar in Columbus looking for the person that did this. He ended up beating the souls out of half the men who were in there, waiting out the storm," he let's out an agitated sigh.

"Is he ok?"

"I don't know, Wade got a call from the owner, and because he's stuck in Tulsa, he sent Cole to check it out. Apparently, when he got there, Garrett had already left. This is gonna need some damage control. I better call Miles." He steps away from me, pressing the phone back to his ear, and I sink down onto the staircase and think about how mad Garrett must be.

What if after all the fighting stops, he blames me?

What if he's got reason to? Was there something more I could have done to help Bill?

I must cry myself to sleep because the next thing I'm aware of is the hand on my shoulder stirring me awake, and I'm surprised when I see Cole staring down at me.

"Come on. Get upstairs and into bed," he tells me in a much softer tone than I expect.

"Did you find him?" I stand up, searching the space around us hopefully, but Cole shakes his head.

"I drove out to the bar, but he's already left. I had to come back, it's gotten real rough out there."

"Why did you come back without him? He's your brother. Why aren't you out there looking for him?" I push past him and head for the door, grabbing the set of keys that are in the bowl.

"Whoa, little lady. I don't think so. No one's going out in that." He opens the door to prove his point, and it almost flies off the hinges. The rain is coming down with such force it rattles the porch roof, and I can see the damage that's already been done. Half the corral's been destroyed, and there's debris all over the yard.

"He can't be out there in that," I shake my head and grip the arm Cole's using to hold me back.

"Garrett's smart; he'd have found shelter. He'll be home

when he's ready. At least try to go to bed. I promise as soon as the storm's cleared, I'll wake ya up, and we'll go looking for him together," he nods his head at Mitch, who comes up from behind us and lifting the collar of his jacket, he holds his hat tight to his head as he rushes out into the storm and back toward the bunkhouse.

"Come on. I need my beauty sleep too," Cole leads me upstairs to my room, and I watch him from my door as he moves on to the room that I assume used to belong to him.

I don't even attempt to sleep. Instead, I sit in my window watching the lightning strike and the rain fill the yard. My eyes don't tire, my heart doesn't stop thumping, and after what seems like forever, I finally see headlights coming up the track.

I stand up and squint my eyes, and when the truck gets close enough for me to be sure it's Garrett's, I spin on my heels and rush down the stairs.

I don't care that the wind almost puts me on my ass when I open the front door. I don't care that the rain soaks my hair and chills my skin. And when Garrett gets out the truck, I don't care that he's covered in blood or worry that he'll reject me.

I launch my body at him, giving him no other option than to catch me when I wrap my arms around his neck. My lips crash onto his and when he pulls me tighter, lifting me onto him, I sense the desperation inside him, too. The rain pelts against our skin as he steps us up onto the porch, and when he forces my back against the front of the house, not even the sky cracking with lightning can distract me from how good it feels to have his tongue dancing around mine.

This is Garrett without restraint, and he feels like heaven and hell combined. His hand pushes the wet hair from my face and holds my cheek in his palm, and for a few seconds, we just stare at each other, catching our breath and standing against the wind.

I'm so scared I'll lose him again, especially since the look on his face is so unreadable.

"I need to get ya inside." He speaks so softly that I almost forget all the questions I have for him, and when I shake my head and kiss him again, he does nothing to stop me. He kisses me back with such force that it drowns out the storm, and I clench my thighs around his waist and grip at his hair to keep me grounded.

"I really have to get you inside," he pulls away breathlessly and carries me in through the door, and when we're inside, and he places me back on my feet, I notice what a bad state he's in.

"Are you hurt?" I look at all the blood on his skin and clothes.

"It's not mine," he shakes his head and takes me by surprise when he grabs my head in both his hands, kissing me again like he's been deprived.

And I don't care that the blood belongs to someone else. I don't care that there's blood at all. I'm learning real quick that Garrett Carson doesn't kiss, he steals your soul, and now I know what that feels like I never want him to stop.

He leads me silently up the stairs to my room, and when he follows me inside, I don't know if it's nerves or excitement that flutter in my stomach.

"Did you kill those men?" I ask, watching him strip the bloody shirt off his shoulders before he comes back at me, gripping my hair and kissing my lips like a starved animal.

"Would you hate me if I did?" He pulls back and waits for my reaction.

"I could never hate you," reaching out my hand, I allow my fingertips to touch his strong chest and feel his heart thump beneath them. Sliding them a little lower, I trail over his abdomen, and when I reach his belt, he grabs both my wrists firmly in his hands and shakes his head.

He kisses me as a distraction, so I take my soaked t-shirt, lift it over my head, and toss it on the floor, making sure he knows I want so much more than his kisses. He squeezes me through my bra with his rough, blood-stained hand, and when I lean my head back, he slides his nose up my neck and leaves a trail of kisses in its path.

"Do you know how much I want you?" he whispers against my skin, stepping us back toward the mattress, then leaning his body over mine until I'm laid down, he finally kisses my lips again.

Having him on top of me causes all that desperation inside of me to swell in my stomach.

"Then have me. I want you, too." I frame his cheeks with both my hands and force his eyes onto mine. I need him to see that I mean it and that I don't have any doubts.

"You're all I want, Garrett, and I want it to be you who takes it…"

Garrett drops his head and sighs.

"I can't," he whispers, and when he looks back up at me, I see the pain on his face, but it doesn't make his words hurt any less.

"Why? Garrett, you feel this. I won't believe that you don't. Tell me what's stopping you." A loud rumble of thunder shakes the house, and the look on his handsome face makes me want to cry.

"Because if I have you, I'll never let you go," he confesses helplessly.

"I'm selfish, I've done some real bad things, and I've hurt a lot of people. I refuse to make you one of them,"

"What if I don't want you to let me go? What if I want to stay here and be with you?" I can feel myself losing him again, and I can't let it happen.

"You'd end up regretting it, and then you'd resent me. You're too young to know what you want from this world, Maisie, and I won't take advantage of that," he pushes himself off the bed and looks down at me shamefully.

"You take that back!" I shoot up and get in his face. "Don't you dare treat me like a fucking kid. I'm a woman with feelings, and you've been fucking with them ever since I got here,"

Garrett takes in what I say without argument, but when I go to slap his face, he quickly grabs my wrist and stops it from impacting.

"I've been protecting you," I can feel his fingers bruising my skin from the tension in them.

"From what, Garrett? Wolves, bears, college boys who spike girl's drinks and home invaders? I grew up in L.A. I've had five different daddies. I'm not some weak helpless…"

"From me," he interrupts. "I've been protecting you from me." His jaw tenses as he swallows all his pride, and when he drops my wrist from his grip and picks up his shirt, he marches for the door and slams it behind him.

CHAPTER 27

GARRETT

I thunder down the stairs and into Pops' office, taking out the bottle of scotch he keeps in his desk. Unscrewing the lid, I knock a mouthful back before taking the seat that used to be his. I can't stop staring at the spot where I last saw him, and it doesn't matter how many men I've killed tonight; the frustration's still there. I should have been here, instead, I was hiding out in the bunkhouse like a fucking pussy, trying to avoid her. The door cracks open, and Cole steps inside, rubbing his hands over his eyes like he just woke up.

"Have all the fun without me?" He smiles sadly, reaching for the bottle when I offer it out.

"Where is he now?" I squeeze my eyes shut to stop 'em from running. Now ain't the time for tears. I'm head of the family, so I gotta show strength.

"They took him to the hospital. Police said they'd come out soon as the storm cleared. I guess it'll buy us some time to figure out a story. How bad is it, Garrett?" He swigs straight from the bottle and takes a seat.

"Three bodies out at Grylls Creek Ranch. I still had enough

sense in me to make it look like a disagreement between them. I'll report Pops' rifle as one of the items stolen."

"Didn't have enough sense in ya to stop yourself from beating the crap outta five men at that bar in Columbus, though, did it?" He's got a judgemental look on his face.

"Someone has to know where he is. A man doesn't just vanish. Besides, we're Carsons, people will expect a reaction, and folk would be more suspicious if I didn't react. Let 'em think that was me seekin' revenge. It gives me an alibi," I shrug, though right now, I couldn't give a fuck if they locked me up and threw away the key. At least it would stop me from chasing Maisie's ass to L.A. when she leaves.

"Mitch called Miles. He'll be here early so we can get the story straight."

"You know anything about an offshore account?" I ask my brother, wondering why Jason and the others didn't take any cash or my mother's old jewelry. It was all scattered on the floor when I arrived. Now I'm thinking straight, this wasn't a revenge attack at all. Jason was looking for something specific, and I wonder where he's been getting his information from. Maybe him being in that bar a few weeks ago was part of the setup.

"No," Cole shakes his head, looking as confused as I am. There ain't no one straighter than Pops. I can't imagine him having any dodgy accounts.

"So what do we do now?" Cole asks, looking around the room where my father spent most of his time.

"We fix all the damage that's been done and get our family its respect back," I light a cigarette with my blood-stained fingers, fingers I should never have touched her with. Hell, I shouldn't have touched her at all. I made her off limits for a reason, and now I've kissed her. I'm doubting if it's gonna be possible to let her leave.

"You gonna miss him?" Cole stares at the same spot I am.

"Yeah, I'll miss him. But men like us don't have time for

grief," I toke back hard and fill my lungs with smoke. "We don't got time for love either," I warn him because once I've hunted down Jason, the Masons will be the next to learn the lesson. Things are gonna change around here, and ruthless things will have to happen. I can't have this family's agenda clouded by his affection for Joe Mason's wife.

"I hear ya, and I'm here for it." Cole stands up.

"But, I'll warn you now. I can see you making the same mistake that I did. And if you think it hurts like this, you wait until she moves on without you," he raises his eyebrows at me before heading out the door, and I pour myself another drink and sink back in the chair.

I guess pain just became my new best friend because no matter how much it hurts, I have to let Maisie Wildman go.

"Whatever it takes," I raise my glass to all the Carson men who are no longer with us, be they in heaven or hell, and hope that when I join them, they'll be grateful for the sacrifice I'm about to make.

CHAPTER 28

MAISIE

I had to shower after Garrett left my room, the blood trails he left on my skin were a reminder of what he's capable of, and the heat he put inside me wasn't cooling down. I barely slept a wink all night, and as soon as the sun rises, I give up trying.

I throw on some yoga pants and an oversized tee and prepare myself to face everything. The police, Mom, him. It all seems so overwhelming.

When I get down the stairs, I'm surprised to see an unfamiliar man dressed in a suit sitting at the dining room table.

"Maisie, I assume?" He stands up and stretches his arm out.

"I'm Miles, the Carson's lawyer,"

"Where's Garrett?" I shake his hand and look around warily. Not only does this guy look far too young to be a lawyer, but I'm not liking the fact there's no sign of Garrett.

"Unfortunately, death doesn't stop a ranch from running. The fences need checking before the herd can be freed, and there's a lot of ground to cover."

"Sounds like you know what you're talking about," I stare back at him blankly.

"My old man used to work in the bunkhouse, and I spent a lot of summers working her,e too,"

"And how does a cowboy become a lawyer?" I question, generally intrigued.

"Hard work and determination, I guess," Miles smiles back at me politely, and I get the feeling I'm not even close to getting the full story on that.

"So, you're here because…?" I take a seat and wait for him to explain himself.

"I can imagine that last night was quite traumatic for you," he starts, sounding like one of the therapists Mom made me see when she thought I'd got too attached to daddy number three.

"I watched my stepfather die and had a gun pointed at me, so that's a pretty accurate assumption," I pout and pour myself water from the jug.

"The police will be here in a few hours to take statements, and you should of course tell them everything you recall," I wait for the but to come. I'm not stupid. I know how much trouble Garrett could be in. "There is a little part of that story I need you to omit," Miles adds.

"Let me guess, the part where Garrett went after them in a murderous rage?" I smile at him cleverly.

"Three of the men have been brought to justice, and I assume you want to protect your stepbrother from any repercussions, that him serving that justice, may cause. I need you to adjust your story a little. You tell the police that Garrett left here with Tate, he's Garrett's alibi. And when they ask what the intruders took, you tell them they took some cash and Bill Carson's rifle. Can you do that, Maisie?" He looks so serious, and maybe even a little hot, staring at me from behind his glasses. I stand up, resting my palms on the table and lean over him.

"I could do that. But you should tell your client if he wants me to lie to the police, then he should have the decency to ask me himself," I keep the stern look on my face as I turn my back and walk away, but on the inside, I feel crushed. Garrett's rejection last night hurt enough, and now this. I've never felt so distant.

I head straight for the shower and turn it on full power. The water hitting my skin reminds me of the way we kissed in the rain last night. It was raw, unfiltered and desperate. Garrett stopped holding back, he let the both of us experience how it could be, and then he took it all away. It's cruel and only proves how selfish he can be.

I let my tears come out while I think about the way he touched me and then how he cast me away. Having his lawyer talk to me on his behalf this morning has to be the final kick in the teeth.

I get out of the shower and wrap myself in a towel, then after brushing my teeth, I head across the landing to my room so I can get dressed.

When I open my door and see Garrett looking out of my bedroom window, I hate the part of me that wants to run to him, and I hate even more that he's put the awkwardness between us that stops me.

"Miles said you wanted to talk to me," he says, but refuses to look at me.

"Sorry for the inconvenience. I just figured if you were gonna ask someone to lie to keep you out of jail, you'd have the decency to ask them yourself," I bite back at him sarcastically as I head to my wardrobe and take out some clean panties. I keep the towel wrapped around me as I pull them up my legs and under my towel, and notice how Garrett's eyes flick between me and the window uncomfortably.

"I didn't know if you'd prefer some space after..." the words get blocked in his mouth, and I drop the towel and fasten on a bra before I step over to the window to join him.

"After you almost fucked me?" I finish his sentence for him, then watch how he heaves a steady breath as his eyes drop between us. And I see the anguish in them before he closes them.

"I would never have fucked you." He glares at me, and I somehow manage to not let his words affect me.

"I don't believe you on that, Garrett. But I will lie for you. I'll tell the police that you left here with Tate, and I'll say those assholes stole your daddy's rifle. Guess you'll have to get out of that bar brawl yourself. But Garrett..." I place my palms on his chest and stretch up on my toes so my mouth touches his ear.

"Don't kid yourself. We both know if I was sticking around, you'd fuck me eventually," I go to walk away, but his firm hand clutches my hip preventing me from going anywhere.

"You better believe it, because it's true. I wouldn't fuck you, Maisie," he drags me closer to his body, and his fingers dig deeper.

"I'd take my time and make sure your first experience was something you'd never forget. I'd worship your body the way it deserves, and I'd make you cum so hard that you'd never want to be taken by anybody else," he growls, looking down his nose at me. "But then I'd have to let you go..." his voice turns weak. "And I won't put either of us through that." When his eyes close, he inhales like he's absorbing me. "You may not understand that right now, but one day you will, and you'll thank me for it. Find someone special, who's worthy of it, but don't ever think that I won't be here wishing it was me." His lips touch my cheek before he walks away, and when he slams my door again, my heart sinks into my stomach, and my tears pour out.

CHAPTER 29

GARRETT

Cora sits in front of the casket, patting a tissue at her crocodile tears. Maisie is beside her, holding her hand, and she keeps glancing in my direction with that sorrowful look on her face. Wade is devastated, but he's trying hard not to show it. I guess that's where I failed as a big brother. I was so determined to stay strong for them I made them think they had to hide their feelings too.

Cole doesn't look sad; he's just angry. And I know neither of my brothers will be forgiving me any time soon for taking those three lives without them.

The case may be closed in the eyes of the law. But it ain't to me. Jason McIntyre is still out there somewhere. Finding him, and making him pay, will be the distraction I need after Maisie leaves for L.A. tomorrow.

Cora refuses to get up from her chair when the service is over. I guess she wants to ensure she plays her grieving widow part right to its bitter end.

It's been a week since Pops died, and yesterday when Miles read out his will, we were all shocked to learn that he'd left her a share in the ranch. It's only a small one, but it ensures that she'll be sticking around.

"Have you thought about what we're gonna do?" Wade asks, as the crowd starts to disperse. Pops ensured I was the one to take over the ranch by leaving the biggest percentage of it to me.

"She ain't gonna sell. I already got Miles to suggest it to her."

"You can't seriously be thinking about letting her stay?" Cole shakes his head as he watches her take comfort from Mayor Walker and his wife.

"Say's the man who still sleeps in the Mason's bunkhouse," Wade pipes up, and before Cole can make a scene and throw a fist at him, I speak up.

"Cole's got his reasons." I stare across the graveyard at Joe Mason and his wife, Aubrey. He's holding her hand as he talks with his father and the Commissioner, and I notice the shy glance she gives my brother.

"We need to stick together. All we got right now is each other's loyalty, and I've figured a way to turn that into power,"

"Now if you could just figure out a way to make her disappear?" Cole gestures his head back towards Cora, who's walking towards us.

"I've invited a few close friends back to the house," she informs me, when she passes on her way to the funeral car. Maisie smiles awkwardly at me as she follows behind with Leia Walker, and Wade takes his hat off for her when she offers him her condolences.

"It's started already. She's gonna strut around like she owns the place," Cole shakes his head.

"And she will if we don't play it carefully," I point out, trying not to show my frustration. "We know how things have gotta be run from now on, we go back to the way things used to be, and laws are gonna have to be broken to get there. But we gotta be smart about it. She'll be waitin' for us to fuck up, because if we ever go down, she gets it all."

"How the fuck we supposed to pull this off with her watchin' our every move?" Wade asks, as we watch Cora get in the car.

"We'll figure it out, but for now, we stay on guard and play nice." Wade and Cole go to join her in the car, and I head over to say one final goodbye to Pops.

"You may not agree with how I'm gonna do things, but I'd like to think that you'll find a way to be proud," I stare down at his casket. "We're gonna make the Carson name what it was, get our ranch back to where it needs to be, and we're gonna need all the help we can get. Keep us in your prayers Pops, and say hi to Bree." I turn and walk away from the grave, placing my hat back on my head before I join the others.

I spend the next few hours being polite to the people Cora invited back to the house. There are way more than just a few, and it's no surprise that she invited all the Masons back here too. Thankfully Pops had the sense to put a clause on her shares so she can't sell them to anyone but us, but I bet the Mason's don't know that. And I can only guess it's the reason their noses are wedged all the way up her ass, right now.

I've had enough of being social, so I head to *my* office, closing the door and pouring myself a drink.

I've already had Miles take care of all of Maisie's college fees. I don't know what Cora's financial situation is, but I'm not willing to bet on her having saved enough to put Maisie through it, and no doubt she was relying on Pops for that. I've also told Miles to make sure she thinks that the $50,000 dollars I had put in her account was left to her by my father. I may not have a place in Maisie Wildman's future, but I'd like to think I can play my part in bettering it.

When the door knocks, I clutch at my glass and hope it ain't her. I'm too weak to be around her right now and seeing her only causes pain.

"Come in," I call out harshly, and when the door opens and old man Mason steps inside, I immediately straighten in my chair.

"Son," he lowers his head, as he steps towards me. I notice that he's taken off his tie and popped open his top button. I also notice the brown file that he carries in his hand.

"What do you want?" I make it clear his company isn't wanted. You know a town is corrupt when your enemies drink your liquor and look far too comfortable in your home.

"I'm expecting you'll be running this place differently to your father," he cuts straight to the chase.

"By not letting you walk all over us," I offer him the same courtesy, and he surprises me when he chuckles.

"We don't need to be enemies, Garrett. In fact I'm here to offer you something. I want to show my gratitude for your recent discretion."

"There is nothing you can offer in return for that. We both know if the Mayor finds out what Caleb does, your relationship is over,"

"Caleb has been reprimanded, and I can assure you that it won't be an issue anymore," The old man is clearly ashamed, and since today don't feel much like a day for victory, I take no pleasure in it.

"I have something for you, information that I think you might appreciate." Placing the file on my desk, he slides it across to me. I have a suspicion that this is what Jason took the night my father died, and I can't help wondering how the fuck it got into Ronnie Mason's hands.

All my suspicions are proved wrong when I open it up and see a picture of my dead sister.

"It's her autopsy report," he confirms, as I stare down at her wide-open eyes and discolored skin. It took the divers three days to find her body after she jumped, and I'll never forget having to be the one who identified her. Pops was too much of a wreck, and I'd never have let my brothers do it.

"I know what it is. Where the *fuck* do you find the business in giving it to me, you sick son of a bitch," I stare across my desk at him, thinking of all the ways I could kill him. It would be poetic justice to hand one of his sons his autopsy report to reveal which one I chose.

"Someone went through a great deal of effort to bury that report, there's no online trace of it, and this paper copy had already been stored in archives. If you turn the page and go to the second paragraph, you'll see why," he gestures his eyes back to the file, and I do as he instructs, turning the page and letting my eyes scan over the words.

Pregnancy gestation 14 weeks.

The words stand out from the page, and I feel the walls close in around me. She can't have been, she was barely sixteen, and Breanna had no interest in boys.

"How did you...?" I look up at Mason and give up on hiding how much of a blow this is.

"Joe doesn't believe in technology, he won't have a computer in the house. About a year ago I caught Aubrey using mine. I had some suspicions, so I had the history checked, and it showed that this report is what she was looking for,"

Aubrey is a lot older than Bree, but our moms were close enough for Aubrey to be the big sister she never had.

"She refused to tell me why, and I'll admit since it involved your family, I took an interest. My intentions at the time weren't exactly neighborly. But I'm hoping that, my giving you this, will set the footing for how we proceed," Mason shows all his cards. He's intimidated by the fact I'm running things now.

"This town never understood why that pretty girl, who had her whole life ahead of her, threw herself off Blackpoint Creek. I don't know who worked so hard to get this buried or who put her in that situation, but I hope you find your answers,"

There's no smugness on his face as he turns away and heads for the door, just pity and sadness.

"This don't mean we're friends," I warn him, before he can leave. My body is shaking with shock, I want to tear down walls, but I have a dignity to uphold.

"I know that. But one good turn deserves another." he nods his head before he leaves, and I read over the words again and again, wondering if they will ever sink in.

I've drunk far too much and locked the report away in my desk drawer. Outside's turned dark, and when I hear the feeble tap on the door, I don't answer. I hope whoever it is will go away. I can't face my brothers yet, I don't know how I'm gonna tell them what I just found out, and when it's Maisie who lets herself in, not one of them, I find myself feeling relieved.

"It's late, everyone's left," She carries a plate of food in her hand and places it on my desk.

"I thought you might want some supper."

"She was pregnant." The words fall out of my mouth because I can't cling to them any longer.

"Who?" Maisie must notice the devastation on my face because she rushes around my desk and on her knees beside me.

"My sister," I explain, still not able to register it myself. It must have been what she was gonna tell me that morning when she came looking for me in the stables. I was too busy to listen, it was calving season, and I wasn't getting any rest back then. She tried to get me to talk with her, and I snapped at her instead.

"I'm sorry." Maisie takes both my hands in hers in an attempt to comfort me.

"She was sixteen. How does that even happen?" More words I don't intend to say slip out as I think about how scared she must have been. She came to me, her big brother, and I told her I was too busy.

"Do you know who the father was?" Maisie asks.

"No idea, but I'll find out." I don't know how yet, but I will. It just became equally as important as killing Jason McIntyre.

"She tried to tell me, and I was too busy," I shake my head and try to hold in my tears. I can't break, not in front of her. Or my brothers. I can't break in front of anyone.

"Don't blame yourself. None of this is your fault." Her words don't mean a thing because it is my fault. If I'd have let her tell me, I'd have found a way to make it ok. I'd have supported her and helped her in all the ways a big brother should.

"Go to bed, Maisie," I tell her robotically, standing up and making my way to the door. I open it for her so she can't argue, and when she gets up off her knees and moves towards me, that urge to grab her and hold her tight makes me grip the edge of the door a little tighter.

"Don't shut me out," she whispers, wrapping her arms around my waist and resting her cheek on my chest. I remain stiff as she holds me, trying my best not to smell her hair and give in to the temptation to squeeze her in my arms and never let her go.

"I have to," my whisper comes out weak and pathetic. "Please, don't make this any harder," There's a desperation in my voice that doesn't belong there. I've never begged for anything in my life, but I'm begging her for this.

"I leave tomorrow morning. I don't want to leave here, never knowing," She looks up at me with those big blue eyes, and I wonder if she'll ever know how much I wanted her.

"I told you, if I have you, I won't let you leave," I warn her again, trying to hold it all together when all I wanna do is give in.

"Then ask me to stay." Those eyes fill up with tears that cascade over her cheeks, and when I wipe one away with the pad of my thumb and can't help bringing it to my lips so I can taste it. I'd have liked to have given her the world, to watch her smile every day and be the cause of all her laughter. But this is the only world I have to offer, and it's too dangerous and far too destroying to keep her in.

"No." My heart cracks from the devastated look I put on her face. Being the cause of her hurt puts a pain inside me that I know won't leave with her, but I'm doing this *for* her.

"You're cursing us both," her bottom lip trembles, and it makes me desperate to kiss it one last time.

"I'm already cursed." I smile back at her sadly, praying to God she'll try to understand. This isn't about her age. Maisie's right, she is a woman. I should never have treated her any different. This is about me doing the right thing and not condemning her to this place or the man I'll have to become to keep it.

"Then I hope that curse follows you to hell, Garrett Carson." She steps away from me, and with all her sadness turned to hate, she does what I asked of her and leaves.

CHAPTER 30
MAISIE

Mom does more crying as she pulls me in for a hug. "Call when you get there," she tells me, as Dalton swings my suitcase into the back of the truck. A few of the bunkhouse boys, including Mitch, have stopped working to say their goodbyes, but there's no sign of Garrett. The fact I haven't burst into tears over that is a miracle.

When Mom's cell sharts to ring, she looks at me awkwardly, and I put her out of her misery.

"Take it. I'll call you when I land." I assure her, and she quickly kisses my cheek before answering it and rushing back inside the house. I hug Mitch, then Finn and figuring that Tate isn't much of a hugger, I nod at him instead.

"You ready?" Dalton jumps into the driver's seat, and when Garrett comes and stands on the porch, dressed the same as he was the first day I saw him, I have a little hope that he's come to say goodbye, too. He nods his head at me as if assuring me one last time that I'm doing the right thing. But nothing about being apart from him feels right.

"Yeah, I'm ready." I manage a smile for Dalton as I step around the truck and jump inside. The truck rumbles when he starts it up, and I keep my eyes on Garrett's as Dalton reverses and pulls us further apart. Garrett stares back at me, his expression neither angry nor sad, and I fight every urge inside me that screams for me to tell Dalton to stop the truck. I close my eyes when the truck turns around, and we start driving down the track that leads to the road. Then when we reach the gate, I flick them open again and see through the wing mirror that Garrett's still watching.

Dalton talks all the way to the airport. I wonder if that's because he knows I'm heartbroken and is trying to distract me or if he's just the most friendly guy I've ever met in my life. When we eventually get there, he pulls up at the drop-off, and gets out to grab my suitcase. I wipe away the lone tear that falls over my cheek, then take a breath before I get out myself.

"Well, I guess I'll be seeing you at Thanksgiving," Dalton smiles.

"No," I shake my head and force back all the tears I want to cry.

"Christmas?" he checks, looking hopeful.

"No. I'm done with this place," I decided last night that if Garrett let me leave I'd never come back. I don't know what we had, but the power of it was overwhelming, and I won't put myself through the pain of losing it again.

"Well you got my number if ya ever need anythin', just holla."

"And if you're ever in L.A…" I laugh just thinking about it. Dalton is a purebred country boy.

"I doubt that, Miss, but it's been a pleasure." He lifts off his hat and kisses my cheek, blushing as he pulls away. Once he's back in the truck, I lift the handle of my suitcase and start wheeling it across the pedestrian crossing toward the terminal.

"Safe travels." He honks the horn and makes me jump when he pulls away, and I find a smile for him as I wave him off.

I'm searching the big screen in the terminal for my flight number when I hear my name, and all that hope I left back at Copper Ridge suddenly floods back into my chest.

I spin around, searching through the people for Garrett, and pain strikes me all over again when it's Wade I see rushing toward me.

"Didn't think I'd let ya leave without saying goodbye, did ya?" he stops and catches his breath, and despite wanting to burst into tears, I smile at him.

"I wondered where you got to last night."

"Chicks dig a grieving man, darlin'," He shrugs unapologetically, then dropping the cheeky grin from his face, he turns serious.

"He's really letting you leave, huh?" his head shakes disapprovingly.

"Looks that way," I let out a disappointed laugh.

"Listen, I know you don't understand his logic right now. But he's doing what he thinks is best for you, and believe me, it'll be hurting him just as much as it is you."

I have nothing to say to that because although I'm mad at him, I take no pleasure in the fact Garrett is hurting too.

"Take care of him," I move closer and wrap my arms around Wade's shoulders, "And tell her how you feel," I whisper before pulling away, and the sad smile he gives me back confirms he won't be taking my advice.

"I'll be seeing you again," he promises.

"You think so?" I laugh.

"I know so. That brother of mine is gonna realize what he's let go, and I can't wait to watch him grovel to get you back."

"Get out of here, Wade." I kiss his cheek and leave him in the terminal, grateful for the friendship we made. And as I walk away to catch the plane back to L.A. and the life I never wanted to leave behind, I feel like a different girl to the one who arrived.

Copper Ridge taught me a lot this summer. I learned how to ride, I learned to find beauty in such simple things, and I learned that love really fucking hurts.

CHAPTER 31

GARRETT

I sit on a log beside the fire and watch the flames dance in the air. The cabin on grid four seems as good a place as any to get this done, and I think of my grandpa as I wait for everyone to arrive.

It's been a week since I let Maisie go, and the pain of it is just as raw. Part of me hopes the pain never goes away because despite the thousands of miles between us, it keeps me close to her.

All that I've sacrificed makes me even more determined to succeed, and I can't do that alone. There's only one way forward, and that's the old way.

"You ready?" Mitch comes out of the cabin holding the branding iron in his hand. I can just about make out the three horses who carry Dalton, Tate and Finn coming towards us from the light the moon provides.

"They're all good men" Mitch tells me like he senses I need some reassurance. "Hank would have picked 'em out, too. It's already in Finn and Dalton's blood and Tate... Well, I don't know what's in his blood. I don't even know if he's fucking human. He's earned his place here, though."

I huff a laugh, watching them get closer and tether up their horses.

"Boss." Finn flicks up the rim of his hat to greet me and takes a spot on the other side of the fire, and when Tate and Dalton join him, I can sense them all wondering why I asked them here. All three of them have proven to me that they can be loyal. It's time to see how far they wanna take that loyalty.

Wade's truck pulls up, and when both him and Cole get out, they look just as confused as each other. I told them a few days ago about the information Mason brought to me, and we're all in agreement on how to handle it.

"What's the problem?" Cole searches around suspiciously.

"Ain't no problem," I assure him,

"You text us both, saying you needed us," Wade stares at me blankly.

"And you're here, which is exactly where you need to be," I light a cigarette and wait for the headlights I can see in the distance, to get closer.

"So you gonna tell us what this is all about?" Wade pipes up again, looking even more confused, when he sees the banged-out old truck rattle up and park beside his, and all three of the River Boys get out. They make their way toward us, and when they're standing around the fire with everyone here, it's time for me to explain.

"You all know about the Carson brand and what it means to take it." I flick my cigarette into the fire.

"What the fuck would they know?" Cole tips his head toward the River Boys. "Pops put a stop to it before they were even a scratch in their daddy's nut sack," he laughs to himself.

"They know enough," I nod my head at Noah, who pulls his

shirt over his head and reveals the brand that I put on his chest a few years ago. And when Sawyer and Zayne do the same, I watch the shock appear on my brother's faces.

"What the fuck?" Wade flicks his eyes between me and them, trying to figure out what he's seeing.

"Couple of years ago, Shelby West came to me and asked for my help. Her grandson and two of his friends had got themselves into some trouble, and she didn't know how to get 'em out of it. I don't need to remind you how good that woman was to us after Mom left?" I tell my brothers, who both nod their heads in agreement, but still look confused as hell.

"So, I did what I had to do. I helped, but I had my concerns."

"What was it you had to do?" Dalton asks with a dumbfounded look on his face.

"He helped us get rid of a body," Noah answers his question for me without a single sign of remorse.

"I knew there were risks, the boys were young and inexperienced, but the man they killed deserved to die."

"That doesn't explain why they got the brand?" Cole frowns, and I can already tell how hurt he is that I kept this from him.

"I was worried that one of them might lose their head, and I figured the best way to make sure that didn't happen was to bind them together."

"And bind them to you?" Wade shakes his disapprovingly. "You know that ain't what the brand's about."

"We took it willingly," Sawyer speaks up. "My grandpa wore the brand. It's the reason my grandma had no doubt about who to go to to get us out the shit. Zayne's pa wore it, too."

Cole stands on his feet and steps around the fire towards them.

"That brand ain't a badge of fucking honour, kid, it's a vow of loyalty and commitment." He jams his finger into Sawyer's chest.

"And have we not shown that commitment?" Sawyer

questions, straightening his back and showing my brother that he won't be intimidated.

"We may work for Mayor Walker, but we take what this means seriously." He assures my brother, and when Cole steps down he turns his anger on me.

"How long you been doing this kind of shit? We're supposed to be a family, and family don't have secrets,"

"Only them, but I'm hoping that's gonna change," I look over the flames at Tate, Finn and Dalton.

"Years ago, Hank Carson branded men who showed him loyalty, he gave them his brand to remind 'em and anyone who crossed 'em that they were protected by our family and its power. We may have lost that power, but I got every intention of getting it back,"

Mitch smiles like a proud father, while Wade and Cole both show their support with a nod of their heads.

"The brand was never there to show who a man belonged to, it was there to show where a man *belonged*, and I invited you three here tonight because there ain't nowhere else you belong more, than here."

The smile on Dalton's face tells me straight away where his head is. I was never in doubt. As a kid, he used to draw the Carson brand on his chest so he could be like his uncle. Finn gives me his answer with a nod of his head. His father wore the brand, and Mitch tells me Davy was a good man. If Finn wants to follow in his footsteps, this is the perfect way to start.

Tate however, is a little harder to read. I don't know his background other than the part about him being in jail. He's friendly enough, but he's got a lone wolf kinda edge to him.

"I'll take your brand, boss," he tells me, showing he's willing by standing up and preparing to go first.

I hand the branding iron back to Mitch, who shoves it into the flames to heat it up. Noah, Zayne and Sawyer watch the three other men get ready to make their vow of loyalty. They'll remember how it feels, and if they don't, the smell of burning flesh will soon remind 'em. They were just scared teenage boys the night I brought them here and made them swear allegiance to me and each other.

"I'm also giving you boys an out." Noah looks surprised when I turn and face them.

"Things are gonna be changing, and anyone who stands in our way will be an enemy. I don't know what your pledge to Mayor Walker is, but if there's a conflict, I'll be expecting a branded man to be on my side of it.

"How you meaning to take it back?" he asks, creasing his eyebrows in confusion.

"I'm telling ya, your dues are paid. You owe me nothing. I'm hoping that promise you made me and each other that night still stands, but if you don't want the brand and the responsibility that comes with it, Mitch gotta blow torch in the cabin,"

"Answer me a question," he looks at me seriously, with Noah, there's no other way.

"Ask it."

"Why haven't you told Walker who supplied the drugs to Tyler?" Noah and the boys are the ones who got the information out of him. "You could really fuck up Mason with that information, get him out of favour and make your life so much easier."

"I could," I nod my head.

"So why haven't you? A smart man would want to be sitting in the Mayor of this town's pocket himself." He shakes his head like he doesn't understand.

"A smart man doesn't want to be sitting in anyone's pocket at all. He wants them sitting in his, and right now, the only pocket Mason's really in is mine. Now let me ask you a more important question?"

"Shoot," Noah looks fearless.

"Why ain't *you* told Walker who supplied the drugs to Tyler?" I ask.

"Guess there's no need for you to ask if that promise still stands," Noah speaks for them all wearing a deadly, serious look on his face. When he first came into town a few years ago, I doubted him, I thought he was the wrong kind of trouble, but he's proved me wrong. I don't know how he got involved in doing the Mayor's dirty work, but right now, I'm looking at it as an advantage. Pops was right about one thing, there is power in politics, I will use it, but I won't be ruled by it.

"We're ready," Mitch takes the brand out of the fire and moves towards Tate. Noah and Sawyer move behind him, and he shoves them away when they each go to take an arm.

"I don't need holding," he tells them both bravely.

"Oh, it ain't for your sake. It's for his," Sawyer nods his head toward Mitch. "When he shoves that thing into your chest, you're gonna wanna throw him into that fire," he smirks.

"In that case, you better help." Tate glances over to Zayne, who steps behind and anchors his arms around his waist while Noah and Sawyer each grab a shoulder.

Tate clamps down on his jaw and waits for the impact. When it comes, his body barely flinches, and he stares at me with eyes like stone as Mitch singes our family brand into his skin.

I nod my gratitude to him when Mitch pulls away and places the brand back in the fire.

"Wasn't that bad, right?" Finn asks nervously, as he pulls off his shirt.

"Had a lot worse," Tate tells him, and I watch Finn's eyes widen with fear as the boys take hold of him and Mitch edges closer.

He stops just before he presses it into his chest, giving him one last chance to back out, and when Finn gives him the nod and squeezes his eyes shut tight, Mitch lets him have it.

The sounds of his deep-throated moan drown out the noise of

sizzling skin, and Noah and Sawyer hold him as he struggles. When Mitch is done, Finn looks down at his chest and blows out a breath, then punches Tate hard in the shoulder.

"You're one fucked up son of a bitch. That hurt like hell."

"Can't know that till ya been there." Tate tips his hat back and sniggers.

"You're next kid," Mitch sounds proud as he reheats the brand.

"I'm ready for it," Dalton nods enthusiastically, stripping out of his shirt and preparing himself. He's a skinny assed fucker, but he's strong, and when Noah and Sawyer move down the line to take his shoulders, he smiles at them gratefully.

"You realize what this means?" Mitch checks, while the iron heats back up.

"I do, sir," he nods back at his uncle. "And I won't let you down... None of you," he looks around at us all.

"I know that," Mitch takes the iron, and nodding for the boys to take some strain, he presses the iron deep into his nephew's skin. Dalton wails so loud it pierces my ears, and when his torture finally finishes, he looks down at his scar with pride.

"Whatever it takes," Mitch nods his head at him bursting with pride, and before he retires the branding iron for the night, I pull him back.

"You're not done yet," I tell him, watching his eyes stretch open with shock when I start to unbutton my shirt.

"That ain't the way, Garrett. Us men brand ourselves to prove our loyalty to you," He's looking at me like I'm crazy, and so are my brothers.

"Well, it's the way *I'm* making it. I won't expect a single man standing around this fire to do anything I ain't prepared to do myself. We wear the brand out of loyalty to each other."

Mitch takes in what I say and smiles as he shoves the iron back into the flames.

When I look over at my brothers, Wade is already up and making his way to stand beside me.

"You get some crazy as shit ideas," he tells me, pulling off his shirt and psyching himself up for the pain.

"How about you, you in?" I ask Cole.

He's been detached since Mom left us. It's the reason he lost his girl to Joe Mason, and he knows it.

"Don't you wanna have something to offer your girl when you get her back?" I ask him, knowing it'll hit a nerve.

"Wade's right, you're fucking crazy," he snarls at me, then stands up and starts stripping out of his shirt.

"I ain't asking you to understand it; I'm asking you to support it," I smirk as I twist his words and throw 'em back at him.

I can't help feeling relieved he's with us on this. Our family history proves that no good comes from division.

"Ready, boss?" Mitch comes at me with the brand, and I tense my body and hold firm when he presses it into my skin. The pain is excruciating, but I withstand it, knowing there's worse to come. And as I watch Mitch brand both my brothers, I already feel some of that power we lost come back.

"I got some beers in the cabin; I say we all celebrate." Mitch taps his nephew on the shoulder, and they head inside to get them, and I leave Wade and Cole talking to Tate and Finn, so I can head over to speak with Noah.

"I know you boys got your own commitments, and I know they come from a lot higher than Mayor Walker." I let the kid know I ain't a fool. "All you gotta do is stay honest with me, and we'll figure everything else out."

"Whatever it takes, right?" Noah pulls his shirt back over his head.

"You ain't stopping for a beer?" I ask, when I notice the other two heading back toward the truck.

"Ain't our kinda party, cowboy, but you know where to find

us." He backs away with a smile on his face that's rarely seen. And when he gets in the passenger seat and Sawyer speeds off, I turn back around and look at my cowboys, my Corrupt Cowboys.

Wade and Finn compare their new scars with Dalton, while Tate and Mitch stand by the fire talking.

"I understand it," Cole steps up beside me and hands me a beer.

"I'm glad about that. It wouldn't be right without you," I huff a laugh and knock it back.

"No, I mean, I understand why you let her go. I did the same thing,"

"And does it still hurt?" I ask, already knowing the answer. Cole working on the Mason's ranch only proves that he ain't afraid of that hurt.

"Every damn day." He tells me honestly. "You're doin' a good thing here; Grandpa would be proud," he adds, taking in the same scene as me.

"*We're* doin' a good thing."

"Just make sure you have someone to do it all for," he taps me on my shoulder and moves to join the others, and I take a little while longer to look at what I got.

I'll sin my way to hell and fight till my knuckles bleed for this ranch. The sacrifice I've made already proves that. I believe in the silent promises that were made here tonight, and for the first time in a real long time, I got hope for the future.

I just can't help wishing that future could include her, too.

EPILOGUE
GARRETT

THREE YEARS LATER

The Dirty Souls club compound isn't what I expected it to be. This isn't some dive bar, it's a complex, and it's evidence that my Uncle Jimmer doesn't do things in half measures.

I get out the truck and head inside, taking a deep breathe and wondering how the fuck this conversation is gonna go down.

After he died, Jimmer didn't show up for Pops' funeral, and I know Mitch would have told him that he'd passed. He makes no secret that the two of them stay in touch. I just gotta hope that the hostility Jimmer had toward my Pops ain't gonna be inherited by me, too.

It's been a long three years since we all took the brand, it's made us stronger, but we've had something holding us back.

Cora fucking Wildman.

Over the years, she's proved just how intolerable she can be. Me and my brothers underestimated her. We expected her to move on to another rich fool. But it turned out she was more resistant then we gave her credit for. She refused to leave the house, even though I built her a cabin of her own. She insisted that we held weekly meetings to keep her updated on her assets, and I've had to explain every damn decision I've made. The bitch ain't stupid, she knows there's things we do below the law, and she's been waiting for that moment when we screw it up.

Yeah, her scrutiny's held us back, it's been frustrating, but now she ain't a problem anymore, and it's time to put all those plans we've been making into action.

That's why I'm here, in Manitou Springs, Colorado, to speak to my Uncle.

I step into a foyer and see a desk with the hooded skull carved into the wood. There's no one around, and so I follow the noise through the double doors into the barroom.

Immediately the chattering stops, and all eyes fall on me.

"Jimmer Carson?" There's no denying which one of them he is. He looks almost identical to grandpa, and before the old man gets a chance to speak, one of his biker buddies is up on his feet, marching towards me.

"Who's asking?" He looks me up and down with an unwelcoming scowl on his pretty-boy face, but I show him no fear. I just calmly raise my hat to greet him.

"Brax, you better hold your old lady back. We gotta real cowboy in the saloon!" I hear one of the big, bearded guys at the bar call out, but I don't take my eyes off the man in front of me.

"You can stand down. I ain't here to cause any trouble," I assure him, fixing my hat back in place before looking past him, to my uncle.

"I don't expect you to recognise me, Uncle Jimmer. It's been a while." I address him directly, and if he's shocked to see me, he shows no evidence of it.

"Which one are ya?" He steps forward and places a hand on his man's shoulder, to ease him off.

"Garrett," I tell him, and the way he nods his head back at

me is scarily familiar. Him and grandpa really were cut from the same cloth.

"Mitch send ya?" he asks, scratching his hand through his stubble.

"No, I came here off my own back." Mitch has been telling me for years that the best way to repair the damage Pops did, is by fixing the Carson chain. Up until now, the last thing I needed was to be affiliated with an outlaw motorcycle club. Cora would have taken a whole lot of pleasure in that. But now that she ain't an issue, I can see where it would have its benefits.

"You wanna step into my office?" He nods his head toward the doors I just stepped through.

"Prez?" The guy beside him has a confused-as-fuck look on his face, but Jimmer shakes his head at him, before leading me back out the door and then into a much smaller barroom that leads off from the foyer.

"So, what can I do for you?" He steps behind the bar and picks up two glasses and a bottle of Jack.

"I wanna take back what my father lost." I figure I might as well get straight to the point. Carson men don't like bullshit, and when he finishes pouring, I pick up the glass he slides over the bar at me. "I got men, good men that I trust," I explain, before knocking it back.

"Mitch tells me you brought back the brand." The smirk on his lips suggests he admires me for it.

"Mitch talks too much," I snigger back at him.

"He's proud, that's why," Jimmer nods. I know the two of them were close before he left. They still are, and I can't help liking the way it feels to hear that.

"So, what do you want from me?" he tops us up again, then looks up at me, waiting for a response.

"I want an ally, someone I know I can trust if the time ever comes," I admit, swirling the liquor around in my glass. It ain't ever easy coming to another man for help, but pride won't stop me from doing what needs to be done.

"And you came to me?" he chuckles to himself.

"If you can't trust family, who can ya?" I shrug my shoulders, making it sound simple.

"Your pa would tell ya different." Jimmer's got a serious look on his face now, one that suggests he's testing me.

"My pa ain't here—I am." I hold his eyes with mine, so he knows how determined I am.

"I know you didn't walk away from the ranch because you didn't care. Grandpa talked about you a lot, and Mitch is always telling his stories. We share the same family history, and we got the same blood running through our veins," I remind him.

"You're right about that, but it still doesn't explain why you're here." He frowns, slouching back in his chair.

"I got some wolves at my door, and I'm prepared to do whatever it takes to protect what our family fought so hard to build. I won't be the Carson that fails, and if that means I have to ask for some help, so be it." I finish what's left in my glass and await his response.

"It's been a long time. My brothers here don't even know that part of me exists." He scratches his jaw again, and if I was playing poker with the man, I'd say it was his tell.

"And yet, the Dirty Dozen was built from it," I remind him of another fact. A man doesn't come to a gunfight without bullets. I've learned all I can about my Uncle Jimmer and this club he adores, since.

"The day I founded this club was the day I left all that behind. Yeah, some branded men followed, but only because they had your grandpa's blessing. We've never looked back, only forward." He makes the words sound like a warning, and I can't tell which way he's gonna go when he stares back at me long and hard.

"I'll help ya," he eventually agrees, keeping his lips straight and that warning look on his face. "But, before you make your deal with the devil, you should know that I got some wolves on my doorstep, too. And if you're an ally of this club, I'll expect to call in some favors of my own,"

"I think I already gotta couple of those favors back on my ranch," I smirk, knowing that Jimmer was the one who called up Mitch and asked him to find a home for Finn, after his old man died. Jimmer's right. This is me making a deal with the devil, but the Souls are the kinda devils you wanna be dancing with instead of fighting, so I hold out my hand to seal that deal, and I get a sense of something real fucking strong when he grips it firmly and shakes. After he's poured us another drink, he looks at me curiously as I bring it to my lips.

"You came all this way just to ask for help?" he narrows his eyes, suspiciously.

"I remember Grandpa always said, if you're man enough to ask for a favor, you should be man enough to face the man you're asking." I smile fondly, when I think of the old man. Uncle Jimmer never came to his funeral, either. Pops said it was because he was a coward, but I've always known differently. "It's a wicked world, and I may be a bad man in it but I'm told, by a man I trust, that me and you share a lot of the same morals. There ain't no need for us to be strangers. If you need me, that's the number you call." I place the ranch's business card on the table and watch my uncle smile when he picks it up.

Finishing my drink, I stand on my feet and get ready to leave.

"Whatever it takes," Jimmer's words make me pause, and he looks up at me with a glisten of pride in his eyes. I'd like to think that wherever he is, Grandpa's witnessing the wrongs that are being righted, here.

"Whatever it takes." I smile and nod my head back at him.

Then lifting my hat in farewell, I head out the door, back toward my truck.

I take a breath once I'm behind the wheel. That went hella better than I expected. But getting the Souls on my side is just the start. There's a whole bunch of crap waiting for me back in Montana, and when I pull down the vizor and take the picture I keep there, of Maisie, out of the note holder, I'm reminded of what's not.

I took the photo from Pops and Cora's wedding album a few days after I let her go. She's wearing that pretty, pink dress, and the photographer's captured her unaware, with the sunset in the background and a smile on her face. I run my thumb over her blonde hair and let myself wonder what she might be doing with herself these days.

Maisie's far too pretty a girl not to have someone in her life, and the thought of her being with that someone, makes me wanna tear my heart out my chest to stop it from hurting. My cell ringing shakes me out of my thoughts, and keeping the photo between my fingers, I quickly answer it with my other hand.

"How'd it go?" Wade shouts, over the chaos in the background.

"As well as it could. We got him on side,"

"That's great fucking news, Garrett," Wade sounds about as relieved as I am.

"You fightin' or fuckin'?" I ask, when I hear moaning in the background.

"I ain't doin' nothin'. Tate's politely reminding a few guys in the bar that it's rude to gossip," he chuckles to himself.

"It's started, then?" It was only a matter of time before word got out.

Cora's body was found last night, and in a small town nothing stays a secret for very long.

"You can't blame the town for thinkin' it, Garrett. You made no secret about the fact you hated her."

"I know, but I ain't the only one who hated her."

"How'd she take it?" I resist putting off asking any longer. Having Wade be the one to call Maisie and break the news was a weak thing to do, and as I look at Maisie's pretty, blue eyes in the picture and how they shine when she smiles, I feel like an asshole for it.

"It was hard to tell her reaction over the phone. But she's coming here for the funeral, next week," he informs me, and I feel that scrape in my chest when his words sink in.

Maisie hasn't been back to Fork River since the day she left for L.A. From what I've heard, she barely spoke to her mother, either. I've regretted letting her go every day, since.

I don't know what I was expecting her to do after she found out Cora had died; I guess I should have seen this coming. But, now that I know she's coming back, there's one thing I can be sure of.

I won't let her go again.

Maisie Wildman belongs with me, and sitting here in my truck, staring at the photo of the woman who owns my heart, I just decided that when it comes to getting her back, there are *no fucking limits*.

ABOUT THE AUTHOR

Come find/stalk me on the following social media platforms.

ACKNOWLEDGMENTS

As always I have to thank my incredible beta team Andrea, Angela, Ellen and Jessica for all their excellent feedback. You girls really know these guys now and I love how you love them, the way I do.

Another huge thank you goes out to Elizabeth and Sophie, for being my final eyes.

To The Soul Sisters (Emma Creed's Dirty Souls). You are an incredible bunch who endlessly support each other, as well as me. And for that, I'm so grateful to each and everyone of you.

To Yvette and Kerry, for all your hard work and being so easy to work with..

And lastly to my incredible family for all your love and support. You guys are my world.

Em x

Printed in Great Britain
by Amazon